CONTEMPORARY AMERICAN FICTION

COMFORT

David Michael Kaplan grew up in western Pennsylvania
and has lived for extended periods in New England,
North Carolina, California, and Iowa, where he's been a
member of the Iowa Writer's Workshop. His fiction has
been published in *The Atlantic*, *The Ohio Review*, and
other magazines, and has been included in *Best American
Short Stories 1986* and in the PEN Syndicated Fiction
Project. He has received writing fellowships from Yaddo;
the Fine Arts Work Center in Provincetown, Massachu-
setts; and the National Endowment for the Arts.
Mr. Kaplan currently lives in Chicago, where he's working on a novel.

COMFORT

David Michael Kaplan

PENGUIN BOOKS

PENGUIN BOOKS
Published by the Penguin Group
Viking Penguin Inc., 40 West 23rd Street,
New York, New York 10010, U.S.A.
Penguin Books Ltd, 27 Wrights Lane,
London W8 5TZ, England
Penguin Books Australia Ltd, Ringwood,
Victoria, Australia
Penguin Books Canada Limited, 2801 John Street,
Markham, Ontario, Canada L3R 1B4
Penguin Books (N.Z.) Ltd, 182–190 Wairau Road,
Auckland 10, New Zealand

Penguin Books Ltd, Registered Offices: Harmondsworth,
Middlesex, England

First published in the United States of America by
Viking Penguin Inc. 1987
Published in Penguin Books 1988

"Doe Season" and "Comfort" first appeared in *The Atlantic;* "Anne Rey" in *The Ohio Review;* "A Mexican Tale" in *New Mexico Humanities Review;* and "Elias Schneebaum" in *Mississippi Review*. "Doe Season" was later reprinted in *The Best American Short Stories 1986*, edited by Raymond Carver with Shannon Ravenel.

"Love, Your Only Mother" and "Tidewater" were selected as
PEN Syndicated Fiction Project Winners.

LIBRARY OF CONGRESS CATALOGING IN PUBLICATION DATA
Kaplan, David Michael.
Comfort.
    Contents: Doe season—Summer people—Love,
your only mother—[etc.]
    I. Title.
[PS3561.A5537C6   1988]   813'.54   87-7344
ISBN 0 14 00.9624 8

Printed in the United States of America by
R. R. Donnelley & Sons Company, Harrisonburg, Virginia
Set in Sabon and Cochin

For my parents,
Sidney and Minnie Marie Kaplan

Acknowledgements

The author wishes to thank the Fine Arts
Work Center in Provincetown, the Yaddo
Corporation, and the Millay Colony for
the Arts for their generous support; The
Henfield Foundation for a Transatlantic
Review Award; and James A. Michener and
the Copernicus Society of America for the
James A. Michener Award.

Contents

Comfort

Doe Season

They were always the same woods, she thought sleepily as they drove through the early morning darkness—deep and immense, covered with yesterday's snowfall which had frozen overnight. They were the same woods that lay behind her house, *and they stretch all the way to here,* she thought, *for miles and miles, longer than I could walk in a day, or a week even, but they are still the same woods.* The thought made her feel good: it was like thinking of God; it was like thinking of the space between here and the moon; it was like thinking of all the foreign countries from her geography book where even now, Andy knew, people were going to bed, while they—she and her father and Charlie Spoon and Mac, Charlie's eleven-year-old son—were driving deeper into the Pennsylvania countryside, to go hunting.

They had risen long before dawn. Her mother, yawning and not trying to hide her sleepiness, cooked them eggs and

1

French toast. Her father smoked a cigarette and flicked ashes into his saucer while Andy listened, wondering *Why doesn't he come?* and *Won't he ever come?*, until at last a car pulled into the graveled drive and honked. "That will be Charlie Spoon," her father said; he always said "Charlie Spoon", even though his real name was Spreun, because Charlie was, in a sense, shaped like a spoon, with a large head and a narrow waist and chest.

Andy's mother kissed her and her father and said, "Well, have a good time" and "Be careful." Soon they were outside in the bitter dark, loading gear by the back-porch light, their breath steaming. The woods behind the house were then only a black streak against the wash of night.

Andy dozed in the car and woke to find that it was half-light. Mac—also sleeping—had slid against her. She pushed him away and looked out the window. Her breath clouded the glass, and she was cold; the car's heater didn't work right. They were riding over gentle hills, the woods on both sides now—the same woods, she knew, because she had been watching the whole way, even while she slept. They had been in her dreams, and she had never lost sight of them.

Charlie Spoon was driving. "I don't understand why she's coming," he said to her father. "How old is she anyway—eight?"

"Nine," her father replied. "She's small for her age."

"So—nine. What's the difference? She'll just add to the noise and get tired besides."

"No, she won't," her father said. "She can walk me to death. And she'll bring good luck, you'll see. Animals—I don't know how she does it, but they come right up to her.

We go walking in the woods, and we'll spot more raccoons
and possums and such than I ever see when I'm alone."

Charlie grunted.

"Besides, she's not a bad little shot, even if she doesn't hunt
yet. She shoots the .22 real good."

"Popgun," Charlie snorted. "And target shooting ain't deer
hunting."

"Well, she's not gonna be shooting anyway, Charlie," her
father said. "Don't worry. She'll be no bother."

"I still don't know why she's coming," Charlie said.

"Because she wants to, and I want her to. Just like you and
Mac. No difference."

Charlie turned onto a side road and after a mile or so
slowed down. "That's it!" he cried. He stopped, backed up,
and entered a narrow dirt road almost hidden by trees. Five
hundred yards down, the road ran parallel to a fenced-in
field. Charlie parked in a cleared area deeply rutted by frozen
tractor tracks. The gate was locked. *In the spring,* Andy
thought, *there will be cows here, and a dog that chases them,*
but now the field was unmarked and bare.

"This is it," Charlie Spoon declared. "Me and Mac was
up here just two weeks ago, scouting it out, and there's deer.
Mac saw the tracks."

"That's right," Mac said.

"Well, we'll just see about that," her father said, putting
on his gloves. He turned to Andy. "How you doing, honeybun?"

"Just fine," she said.

Andy shivered and stamped as they unloaded: first the
rifles, which they unsheathed and checked, sliding the bolts,

sighting through scopes, adjusting the slings; then the gear, their food and tents and sleeping bags and stove stored in four backpacks—three big ones for Charlie Spoon and her father and Mac, and a day pack for her.

"That's about your size," Mac said, to tease her.

She reddened and said, "Mac, I can carry a pack big as yours any day." He laughed and pressed his knee against the back of hers, so that her leg buckled. "Cut it out," she said. She wanted to make an iceball and throw it at him, but she knew that her father and Charlie were anxious to get going, and she didn't want to displease them.

Mac slid under the gate, and they handed the packs over to him. Then they slid under and began walking across the field toward the same woods that ran all the way back to her home, where even now her mother was probably rising again to wash their breakfast dishes and make herself a fresh pot of coffee. *She is there, and we are here:* the thought satisfied Andy. There was no place else she would rather be.

Mac came up beside her. "Over there's Canada," he said, nodding toward the woods.

"Huh!" she said. "Not likely."

"I don't mean *right* over there. I mean further up north. You think I'm dumb?"

Dumb as your father, she thought.

"Look at that," Mac said, pointing to a piece of cow dung lying on a spot scraped bare of snow. "A frozen meadow muffin." He picked it up and sailed it at her. "Catch!"

"Mac!" she yelled. His laugh was as gawky as he was. She walked faster. He seemed different today somehow, bundled in his yellow-and-black-checkered coat, a rifle in hand, his silly floppy hat not quite covering his ears. They all seemed

different as she watched them trudge through the snow—
Mac and her father and Charlie Spoon—bigger, maybe, as
if the cold landscape enlarged rather than diminished them,
so that they, the only figures in that landscape, took on size
and meaning just by being there. If they weren't there, everything would be quieter, and the woods would be the same as
before. *But they are here,* Andy thought, looking behind her
at the boot prints in the snow, *and I am too, and so it's all
different.*

"We'll go down to the cut where we found those deer
tracks," Charlie said as they entered the woods. "Maybe we'll
get lucky and get a late one coming through."

The woods descended into a gully. The snow was softer
and deeper here, so that often Andy sank to her knees. Charlie
and Mac worked the top of the gully while she and her father
walked along the base some thirty yards behind them. "If
they miss the first shot, we'll get the second," her father said,
and she nodded as if she had known this all the time. She
listened to the crunch of their boots, their breathing, and the
drumming of a distant woodpecker. And the crackling. In
winter the woods crackled as if everything were straining,
ready to snap like dried chicken bones.

We are hunting, Andy thought. The cold air burned her
nostrils.

They stopped to make lunch by a rock outcropping that
protected them from the wind. Her father heated the bean
soup her mother had made for them, and they ate it with
bread already stiff from the cold. He and Charlie took a few
pulls from a flask of Jim Beam while she scoured the plates
with snow and repacked them. Then they had coffee with
sugar and powdered milk, and her father poured her a cup,

too. "We won't tell your momma," he said, and Mac laughed. Andy held the cup the way her father did, not by the handle but around the rim. The coffee tasted smoky. She felt a little queasy, but she drank it all.

Charlie Spoon picked his teeth with a fingernail. "Now, you might've noticed one thing," he said.

"What's that?" her father asked.

"You might've noticed you don't hear no rifles. That's because there ain't no other hunters here. We've got the whole damn woods to ourselves. Now, I ask you—do I know how to find 'em?"

"We haven't seen deer yet, neither."

"Oh, we will," Charlie said, "but not for a while now." He leaned back against the rock. "Deer're sleeping, resting up for the evening feed."

"I seen a deer behind our house once, and it was afternoon," Andy said.

"Yeah, honey, but that was *before* deer season," Charlie said, grinning. "They know something now. They're smart that way."

"That's right," Mac said.

Andy looked at her father—had she said something stupid?

"Well, Charlie," he said, "if they know so much, how come so many get themselves shot?"

"Them's the ones that don't *believe* what they know," Charlie replied. The men laughed. Andy hesitated, and then laughed with them.

They moved on, as much to keep warm as to find a deer. The wind became even stronger. Blowing through the tree-tops, it sounded like the ocean, and once Andy thought she could smell salt air. But that was impossible; the ocean was *hundreds* of miles away, farther than Canada even. She and her parents had gone last summer to stay for a week at a motel on the New Jersey shore. That was the first time she'd seen the ocean, and it frightened her. It was huge and empty, yet always moving. Everything lay hidden. If you walked in it, you couldn't see how deep it was or what might be below; if you swam, something could pull you under and you'd never be seen again. Its musky, rank smell made her think of things dying. Her mother had floated beyond the breakers, calling to her to come in, but Andy wouldn't go farther than a few feet into the surf. Her mother swam and splashed with animal-like delight while her father, smiling shyly, held his white arms above the waist-deep water as if afraid to get them wet. Once a comber rolled over and sent them both tossing, and when her mother tried to stand up, the surf receding behind, Andy saw that her mother's swimsuit top had come off, so that her breasts swayed free, the nipples like two dark eyes. Embarrassed, Andy looked around: except for two women under a yellow umbrella farther up, the beach was empty. Her mother stood up unsteadily, regained her footing. Taking what seemed the longest time, she calmly refixed her top. Andy lay on the beach towel and closed her eyes. The sound of the surf made her head ache.

And now it was winter; the sky was already dimming, not just with the absence of light but with a mist that clung to the hunters' faces like cobwebs. They made camp early. Andy was chilled. When she stood still, she kept wiggling her toes to make sure they were there. Her father rubbed her arms and held her to him briefly, and that felt better. She unpacked the food while the others put up the tents.

"How about rounding us up some firewood, Mac?" Charlie asked.

"I'll do it," Andy said. Charlie looked at her thoughtfully and then handed her the canvas carrier.

There wasn't much wood on the ground, so it took her a while to get a good load. She was about a hundred yards from camp, near a cluster of high, lichen-covered boulders, when she saw through a crack in the rock a buck and two does walking gingerly, almost daintily, through the alder trees. She tried to hush her breathing as they passed not more than twenty yards away. There was nothing she could do. If she yelled, they'd be gone; by the time she got back to camp, they'd be gone. The buck stopped, nostrils quivering, tail up and alert. He looked directly at her. Still she didn't move, not one muscle. He was a beautiful buck, the color of late-turned maple leaves. Unafraid, he lowered his tail, and he and his does silently merged into the trees. Andy walked back to camp and dropped the firewood.

"I saw three deer," she said. "A buck and two does."

"Where?" Charlie Spoon cried, looking behind her as if they might have followed her into camp.

"In the woods yonder. They're gone now."

"Well, hell!" Charlie banged his coffee cup against his knee.

"Didn't I say she could find animals?" her father said, grinning.

"Too late to go after them," Charlie muttered. "It'll be dark in a quarter hour. Damn!"

"Damn," Mac echoed.

"They just walk right up to her," her father said.

"Well, leastwise this proves there's deer here." Charlie began snapping long branches into shorter ones. "You know, I think I'll stick with you," he told Andy, "since you're so good at finding deer and all. How'd that be?"

"Okay, I guess," Andy murmured. She hoped he was kidding: no way did she want to hunt with Charlie Spoon. Still, she was pleased he had said it.

Her father and Charlie took one tent, she and Mac the other. When they were in their sleeping bags, Mac said in the darkness, "I bet you really didn't see no deer, did you?"

She sighed. "I did, Mac. Why would I lie?"

"How big was the buck?"

"Four point. I counted."

Mac snorted.

"You just believe what you want, Mac," she said testily.

"Too bad it ain't buck season," he said. "Well, I got to go pee."

"So pee."

She heard him turn in his bag. "You ever see it?" he asked.

"It? What's 'it'?"

"It. A pecker."

"Sure," she lied.

"Whose? Your father's?"

She was uncomfortable. "No," she said.

"Well, whose, then?"

"Oh, I don't know! Leave me be, why don't you?"

"Didn't see a deer, didn't see a pecker," Mac said teasingly.

She didn't answer right away. Then she said, "My cousin Lewis. I saw his."

"Well, how old's he?"

"One and a half."

"Ha! A baby! A baby's is like a little worm. It ain't a real one at all."

If he says he'll show me his, she thought, *I'll kick him. I'll just get out of my bag and kick him.*

"I went hunting with my daddy and Versh and Danny Simmons last year in buck season," Mac said, "and we got ourselves one. And we hog-dressed the thing. You know what that is, don't you?"

"No," she said. She was confused. What was he talking about now?

"That's when you cut him open and take out all his guts, so the meat don't spoil. Makes him lighter to pack out, too."

She tried to imagine what the deer's guts might look like, pulled from the gaping hole. "What do you do with them?" she asked. "The guts?"

"Oh, just leave 'em for the bears."

She ran her finger like a knife blade along her belly.

"When we left them on the ground," Mac said, "they smoked. Like they were cooking."

"Huh," she said.

"They cut off the deer's pecker, too, you know."

Andy imagined Lewis's pecker and shuddered. "Mac, you're disgusting."

He laughed. "Well, I gotta go pee." She heard him rustle out of his bag. "Broo!" he cried, flapping his arms. "It's cold!"

He makes so much noise, she thought, *just noise and more noise.*

Her father woke them before first light. He warned them to talk softly and said that they were going to the place where Andy had seen the deer, to try to cut them off on their way back from their night feeding. Andy couldn't shake off her sleep. Stuffing her sleeping bag into its sack seemed to take an hour, and tying her boots was the strangest thing she'd ever done. Charlie Spoon made hot chocolate and oatmeal with raisins. Andy closed her eyes and, between beats of her heart, listened to the breathing of the forest. *When I open my eyes, it will be lighter,* she decided. But when she did, it was still just as dark, except for the swaths of their flashlights and the hissing blue flame of the stove. *There has to be just one moment when it all changes from dark to light,* Andy thought. She had missed it yesterday, in the car; today she would watch more closely.

But when she remembered again, it was already first light and they had moved to the rocks by the deer trail and had set up shooting positions—Mac and Charlie Spoon on the up-trail side, she and her father behind them, some six feet up on a ledge. The day became brighter, the sun piercing the tall pines, raking the hunters, yet providing little warmth. Andy now smelled alder and pine and the slightly rotten odor of rock lichen. She rubbed her hand over the stone and con- sidered that it must be very old, had probably been here before the giant pines, *before anyone was in these woods at all.* A chipmunk sniffed on a nearby branch. She aimed an imagi- nary rifle and pressed the trigger. The chipmunk froze, then scurried away. Her legs were cramping on the narrow ledge. Her father seemed to doze, one hand in his parka, the other cupped lightly around the rifle. She could smell his scent of old wool and leather. His cheeks were speckled with gray- black whiskers, and he worked his jaws slightly, as if chewing a small piece of gum.

Please let us get a deer, she prayed.

A branch snapped on the other side of the rock face. Her father's hand stiffened on the rifle, startling her—*He hasn't been sleeping at all,* she marveled—and then his jaw relaxed, as did the lines around his eyes, and she heard Charlie Spoon call, "Yo, don't shoot, it's us." He and Mac appeared from around the rock. They stopped beneath the ledge. Charlie solemnly crossed his arms.

"I don't believe we're gonna get any deer here," he said drily.

Andy's father lowered his rifle to Charlie and jumped down from the ledge. Then he reached up for Andy. She dropped into his arms and he set her gently on the ground.

Mac sidled up to her. "I knew you didn't see no deer," he said.

"Just because they don't come when you want 'em to don't mean she didn't see them," her father said.

Still, she felt bad. Her telling about the deer had caused them to spend the morning there, cold and expectant, with nothing to show for it.

They tramped through the woods for another two hours, not caring much about noise. Mac found some deer tracks, and they argued about how old they were. They split up for a while and then rejoined at an old logging road that deer might use, and followed it. The road crossed a stream, which had mostly frozen over but in a few spots still caught leaves and twigs in an icy swirl. They forded it by jumping from rock to rock. The road narrowed after that, and the woods thickened.

They stopped for lunch, heating up Charlie's wife's corn chowder. Andy's father cut squares of applesauce cake with his hunting knife and handed them to her and Mac, who ate his almost daintily. Andy could faintly taste knife oil on the cake. She was tired. She stretched her leg; the muscle that had cramped on the rock still ached.

"Might as well relax," her father said, as if reading her thoughts. "We won't find deer till suppertime."

Charlie Spoon leaned back against his pack and folded his hands across his stomach. "Well, even if we don't get a deer," he said expansively, "it's still great to be out here, breathe some fresh air, clomp around a bit. Get away from the house and the old lady." He winked at Mac, who looked away.

"That's what the woods are all about, anyway," Charlie said. "It's where the women don't want to go." He bowed his head toward Andy. "With your exception, of course, little lady." He helped himself to another piece of applesauce cake.

"She ain't a woman," Mac said.

"Well, she damn well's gonna be," Charlie said. He grinned at her. "Or will you? You're half a boy anyway. You go by a boy's name. What's your real name? Andrea, ain't it?"

"That's right," she said. She hoped that if she didn't look at him, Charlie would stop.

"Well, which do you like? Andy or Andrea?"

"Don't matter," she mumbled. "Either."

"She's always been Andy to me," her father said.

Charlie Spoon was still grinning. "So what are you gonna be, Andrea? A boy or a girl?"

"I'm a girl," she said.

"But you want to go hunting and fishing and everything, huh?"

"She can do whatever she likes," her father said.

"Hell, you might as well have just had a boy and be done with it!" Charlie exclaimed.

"That's funny," her father said, and chuckled. "That's just what her momma tells me."

They were looking at her, and she wanted to get away from them all, even from her father, who chose to joke with them.

"I'm going to walk a bit," she said.

She heard them laughing as she walked down the logging trail. She flapped her arms; she whistled. *I don't care how much noise I make,* she thought. Two grouse flew from the underbrush, startling her. A little farther down, the trail ended in a clearing that enlarged into a frozen meadow; beyond it the woods began again. A few moldering posts were all that was left of a fence that had once enclosed the field. The low afternoon sunlight reflected brightly off the snow, so that Andy's eyes hurt. She squinted hard. A gust of wind blew across the field, stinging her face. And then, as if it had been waiting for her, the doe emerged from the trees opposite and stepped cautiously into the field. Andy watched: it stopped and stood quietly for what seemed a long time and then ambled across. It stopped again about seventy yards away and began to browse in a patch of sugar grass uncovered by the wind. Carefully, slowly, never taking her eyes from the doe, Andy walked backward, trying to step into the boot prints she'd already made. When she was far enough back into the woods, she turned and walked faster, her heart racing. *Please let it stay,* she prayed.

"There's a doe in the field yonder," she told them.

They got their rifles and hurried down the trail.

"No use," her father said. "We're making too much noise any way you look at it."

"At least we got us the wind in our favor," Charlie Spoon said, breathing heavily.

But the doe was still there, grazing.

"Good Lord," Charlie whispered. He looked at her father. "Well, whose shot?"

"Andy spotted it," her father said in a low voice. "Let her shoot it."

"What!" Charlie's eyes widened.

Andy couldn't believe what her father had just said. She'd only shot tin cans and targets; she'd never even fired her father's .30–30, and she'd never killed anything.

"I can't," she whispered.

"That's right, she can't," Charlie Spoon insisted. "She's not old enough and she don't have a license even if she was!"

"Well, who's to tell?" her father said. "Nobody's going to know but us." He looked at her. "Do you want to shoot it, punkin?"

Why doesn't it hear us? she wondered. *Why doesn't it run away?* "I don't know," she said.

"Well, I'm sure as hell gonna shoot it," Charlie said. Her father grasped Charlie's rifle barrel and held it. His voice was steady.

"Andy's a good shot. It's her deer. She found it, not you. You'd still be sitting on your ass back in camp." He turned to her again. "Now—do you want to shoot it, Andy? Yes or no."

He was looking at her; they were all looking at her. Suddenly she was angry at the deer, who refused to hear them, who wouldn't run away even when it could. "I'll shoot it," she said. Charlie turned away in disgust.

She lay on the ground and pressed the rifle stock against her shoulder bone. The snow was cold through her parka; she smelled oil and wax and damp earth. She pulled off one glove with her teeth. "It sights just like the .22," her father said gently. "Cartridge's already chambered." As she had done so many times before, she sighted down the scope; now the doe was in the reticle. She moved the barrel until the cross hairs lined up. Her father was breathing beside her.

"Aim where the chest and legs meet, or a little above, punkin," he was saying calmly. "That's the killing shot."

But now, seeing it in the scope, Andy was hesitant. Her finger weakened on the trigger. Still, she nodded at what her father said and sighted again, the cross hairs lining up in exactly the same spot—the doe had hardly moved, its brownish gray body outlined starkly against the blue-backed snow. *It doesn't know,* Andy thought. *It just doesn't know.* And as she looked, deer and snow and faraway trees flattened within the circular frame to become like a picture on a calendar, not real, and she felt calm, as if she had been dreaming everything—the day, the deer, the hunt itself. And she, finger on trigger, was only a part of that dream.

"Shoot!" Charlie hissed.

Through the scope she saw the deer look up, ears high and straining.

Charlie groaned, and just as he did, and just at the moment when Andy knew—*knew*—the doe would bound away, as if she could feel its haunches tensing and gathering power, she pulled the trigger. Later she would think, *I felt the recoil, I smelled the smoke, but I don't remember pulling the trigger.* Through the scope the deer seemed to shrink into itself, and then slowly knelt, hind legs first, head raised as if to cry out. It trembled, still straining to keep its head high, as if that alone would save it; failing, it collapsed, shuddered, and lay still.

"Whoee!" Mac cried.

"One shot! One shot!" her father yelled, clapping her on the back. Charlie Spoon was shaking his head and smiling dumbly.

"I told you she was a great little shot!" her father said. "I told you!" Mac danced and clapped his hands. She was dazed, not quite understanding what had happened. And then they were crossing the field toward the fallen doe, she walking dreamlike, the men laughing and joking, released now from the tension of silence and anticipation. Suddenly Mac pointed and cried out, "Look at that!"

The doe was rising, legs unsteady. They stared at it, unable to comprehend, and in that moment the doe regained its feet and looked at them, as if it, too, were trying to understand. Her father whistled softly. Charlie Spoon unslung his rifle and raised it to his shoulder, but the doe was already bounding away. His hurried shot missed, and the deer disappeared into the woods.

"Damn, damn, damn," he moaned.

"I don't believe it," her father said. "That deer was dead."

"Dead, hell!" Charlie yelled. "It was gutshot, that's all. Stunned and gutshot. Clean shot, my ass!"

What have I done? Andy thought.

Her father slung his rifle over his shoulder. "Well, let's go. She can't get too far."

"Hell, I've seen deer run ten miles gutshot," Charlie said. He waved his arms. "We may never find her!"

As they crossed the field, Mac came up to her and said in a low voice, "Gutshoot a deer, you'll go to hell."

"Shut up, Mac," she said, her voice cracking. It was a terrible thing she had done, she knew. She couldn't bear to think of the doe in pain and frightened. *Please let it die,* she prayed.

But though they searched all the last hour of daylight, so that they had to recross the field and go up the logging trail in a twilight made even deeper by thick, smoky clouds, they didn't find the doe. They lost its trail almost immediately in the dense stands of alderberry and larch.

"I am cold, and I am tired," Charlie Spoon declared. "And if you ask me, that deer's in another county already."

"No one's asking you, Charlie," her father said.

They had a supper of hard salami and ham, bread, and the rest of the applesauce cake. It seemed a bother to heat the coffee, so they had cold chocolate instead. Everyone turned in early.

"We'll find it in the morning, honeybun," her father said, as she went to her tent.

"I don't like to think of it suffering." She was almost in tears.

"It's dead already, punkin. Don't even think about it." He kissed her, his breath sour and his beard rough against her cheek.

Andy was sure she wouldn't get to sleep; the image of the doe falling, falling, then rising again, repeated itself whenever she closed her eyes. Then she heard an owl hoot and realized that it had awakened her, so she must have been asleep after all. She hoped the owl would hush, but instead it hooted louder. She wished her father or Charlie Spoon would wake up and do something about it, but no one moved in the other tent, and suddenly she was afraid that they had all decamped, wanting nothing more to do with her. She whispered, "Mac, Mac," to the sleeping bag where he should be, but no one answered. She tried to find the flashlight she always kept by her side, but couldn't, and she cried in panic, "Mac, are you there?" He mumbled something, and immediately she felt foolish and hoped he wouldn't reply.

When she awoke again, everything had changed. The owl was gone, the woods were still, and she sensed light, blue and pale, light where before there had been none. *The moon must have come out,* she thought. And it was warm, too, warmer than it should have been. She got out of her sleeping bag and took off her parka—it was that warm. Mac was asleep, wheezing like an old man. She unzipped the tent and stepped outside.

The woods were more beautiful than she had ever seen them. The moon made everything ice-rimmed glimmer with a crystallized, immanent light, while underneath that ice the branches of trees were as stark as skeletons. She heard a crunching in the snow, the one sound in all that silence, and there, walking down the logging trail into their camp, was the doe. Its body, like everything around her, was silvered with frost and moonlight. It walked past the tent where her father and Charlie Spoon were sleeping and stopped no more than six feet from her. Andy saw that she had shot it, yes, had shot it cleanly, just where she thought she had, the wound a jagged, bloody hole in the doe's chest.

A heart shot, she thought.

The doe stepped closer, so that Andy, if she wished, could have reached out and touched it. It looked at her as if expecting her to do this, and so she did, running her hand, slowly at first, along the rough, matted fur, then down to the edge of the wound, where she stopped. The doe stood still. Hesitantly, Andy felt the edge of the wound. The torn flesh was sticky and warm. The wound parted under her touch. And then, almost without her knowing it, her fingers were within, probing, yet still the doe didn't move. Andy pressed deeper, through flesh and muscle and sinew, until her whole hand and more was inside the wound and she had found the doe's heart, warm and beating. She cupped it gently in her hand. *Alive,* she marveled. *Alive.*

The heart quickened under her touch, becoming warmer and warmer until it was hot enough to burn. In pain, Andy tried to remove her hand, but the wound closed about it and held her fast. Her hand was burning. She cried out in agony, sure they would all hear and come help, but they didn't. And then her hand pulled free, followed by a steaming rush of blood, more blood than she ever could have imagined—it covered her hand and arm, and she saw to her horror that her hand was steaming. She moaned and fell to her knees and plunged her hand into the snow. The doe looked at her gently and then turned and walked back up the trail.

In the morning, when she woke, Andy could still smell the blood, but she felt no pain. She looked at her hand. Even though it appeared unscathed, it felt weak and withered. She couldn't move it freely and was afraid the others would notice. *I will hide it in my jacket pocket,* she decided, *so nobody can see.* She ate the oatmeal that her father cooked and stayed apart from them all. No one spoke to her, and that suited her. A light snow began to fall. It was the last day of their hunting trip. She wanted to be home.

Her father dumped the dregs of his coffee. "Well, let's go look for her," he said.

Again they crossed the field. Andy lagged behind. She

averted her eyes from the spot where the doe had fallen, already filling up with snow. Mac and Charlie entered the woods first, followed by her father. Andy remained in the field and considered the smear of gray sky, the nearby flock of crows pecking at unyielding stubble. *I will stay here,* she thought, *and not move for a long while.* But now someone— Mac—was yelling. Her father appeared at the woods' edge and waved for her to come. She ran and pushed through a brake of alderberry and larch. The thick underbrush scratched her face. For a moment she felt lost and looked wildly about. Then, where the brush thinned, she saw them standing quietly in the falling snow. They were staring down at the dead doe. A film covered its upturned eye, and its body was lightly dusted with snow.

"I told you she wouldn't get too far," Andy's father said triumphantly. "We must've just missed her yesterday. Too blind to see."

"We're just damn lucky no animal got to her last night," Charlie muttered.

Her father lifted the doe's foreleg. The wound was blood-clotted, brown, and caked like frozen mud. "Clean shot," he said to Charlie. He grinned. "My little girl."

Then he pulled out his knife, the blade gray as the morning. Mac whispered to Andy, "Now watch this," while Charlie Spoon lifted the doe from behind by its forelegs so that its head rested between his knees, its underside exposed. Her father's knife sliced thickly from chest to belly to crotch, and Andy was running from them, back to the field and across, scattering the crows who cawed and circled angrily. And now they were all calling to her—Charlie Spoon and Mac and her father—crying *Andy, Andy* (but that wasn't her name, she would no longer be called that); yet louder than any of them was the wind blowing through the treetops, like the ocean where her mother floated in green water, also calling *Come in, come in,* while all around her roared the mocking of the terrible, now inevitable, sea.

Summer People

---

*F*rank and his father drove up to the lake at the end of the season, long after the summer people—including those who had rented the house—had returned to their real homes, taking with them their grills and motorboats and deck chairs and water skis. It was an early October morning. A milky haze—the ghost of an earlier fog—hung over the lake, and the trees loomed grayish green, half-water, half-air. His father parked on the dead grass behind the summer house. Geese honked from somewhere within the haze.

"We're here," his father announced.

Neither of them moved to get out. Frank sipped the coffee, already lukewarm, that they'd bought in the country store down at the turnoff. His father rolled down the window and breathed deeply.

"Chilly," he noted.

The blue spruce and pine surrounding the house seemed

much larger than Frank remembered—*but then they would be, wouldn't they,* he thought—while the house itself seemed smaller. His father had recently repainted it the same light green as always, although Frank remembered the shutters as white, not brown.

"I'm going to repaint it," he'd told Frank in a phone call early that summer. "And then I'm going to sell it."

"Do you really want to do that?" Frank asked.

"It's hardly worth the trouble of keeping it up. I don't go there anymore, what with your mother gone. And I'm tired of renting it—all I do is worry about it all summer." He paused. "And you never use it. You haven't been there in years."

Fourteen years, Frank thought. During that time he'd graduated from college, moved to three different states in pursuit of a career that had never quite taken shape, married Jena, and—most recently—divorced her.

In early August his father had called again.

"I think I've sold it," he told Frank.

"That's good," Frank said.

"They're a real nice family. They've got a boy about the age you were when we first went up there."

And still later, in mid-September, his father surprised Frank by asking him to come help close up the house for the season.

"It's in escrow right now," he explained. "So I've still got to do it this year."

"Dad, I'm four hundred miles away. What's wrong with the boy you've been hiring?"

"I want to do a really good job for these new people," his father said.

"I don't know," Frank said. "Things are busy now."

"Besides, we don't see each other much anymore."

Frank said nothing.

"It's the last year," his father said. "Please."

Frank hesitated, then agreed.

"But I don't want to argue," he said. "No arguments."

"Not from me," his father had reassured him.

Across the lake the geese now skirred the water and flew away. His father opened the car door and threw the last of his coffee on the ground, where it steamed.

"Well, it's a good day for doing it," he said. "Last year it was cold as hell."

While his father unlocked the cellar to find the tools they'd need, Frank walked, hands in pockets, to the dock and stared into the mist. Wavelets lapped the pilings. A foamy scum of decaying leaves and algae ringed the bank, which curved in close by the dock to form a small cove. Frank lay on his stomach and dipped his hand into the water. *Cold as ever.* He stood up, and saw the rope dangling from the huge oak that jutted out over the cove.

"I'll be damned," he murmured.

His father came up behind him.

"That's the rope you hung for me to swing from," Frank said.

His father squinted. "Sure."

"I can't believe it's still there. Why hasn't it rotted away?"

"It's heavy rope. Oiled."

The rope fell past a large oak limb some twenty-five feet above the water. That had been the jumping-off point. As a boy, Frank had climbed to it on the boards his father had nailed into the trunk of the tree. Grasping the rope before swinging out, he would stare down at the water, which seemed to stare back at him, dark and judgmental and waiting.

"It was scary how high that was," Frank said.

"Really?"

"You put it pretty high, Dad," Frank said. "Believe me."

His father looked. "It's not that high."

They walked back to the house. His father took a key from his ring and turned the lock. The door wouldn't open. He jiggled the key, pulled hard on the door, and turned the key again.

"Lock gets worse every year," he muttered. He jiggled the key harder. The door opened.

"I've got to replace it," he said.

"Let the other folks worry about it, Dad," Frank said. His father looked puzzled. "I mean, it's not going to be your worry anymore, is it?"

They opened the shades, and diffused morning light poured into the front room. Much of the furniture seemed different, though just as worn and old as any Frank could remember. The print of *Lake Leman by Moonlight* still hung in its cracked glass frame over the fireplace, and the ugly driftwood lamp, a purchase from a childhood trip to Florida, still adorned the end table. As a boy, Frank had stared at the pockmarks in the driftwood, waiting for the worms that he was sure lived inside to emerge. The smell of pine and must was what seemed most familiar—that and the smell of the lake, raw and brackish, which had always been stronger here than down at water's edge.

"Still seem the same?" his father asked.

"Sort of."

His father went upstairs to inspect, and Frank walked into the kitchen. The sun had come out now, and its light through the drawn window shades tinted the room golden-brown. He opened the refrigerator: it was empty, and clean, as were the cupboards. Above him the floorboards creaked as his father walked through the upstairs rooms opening closet doors, window shutters, and bureau drawers. Frank pulled up a window shade. The haze was rapidly lifting from the lake, and a breeze gently stirred the trees and dimpled the water. His father came back downstairs.

"The kitchen looks good," Frank said.

His father inspected the refrigerator, then the freezer. "They defrosted it," he said in wonder. "On the last season, I finally get some decent renters." He sat down at the kitchen table. "One year people left some Coke bottles in the freezer, and they exploded all over the damn place." He picked up a salt shaker and turned it over in his fingers. "Another year, your mother and I found all the porch chairs in the closet, broken up and stacked like kindling. Can you believe it?" He tipped the shaker, and a little salt fell on the table. He carefully swept it into his palm. "People just don't care."

"Maybe we should get started, Dad," Frank suggested.

"What's the hurry? We've got all day." His father unscrewed the top of the shaker and brushed the salt back inside. "Let's take it easy, do a good job, then go have a nice dinner somewhere." He wiped his hands on his pants.

"So—what do you want me to do?" Frank asked.

His father folded his hands and seemed not to hear him.

"Dad?"

"You're not sorry I sold it, are you?" his father asked.

"The house? Why should I be?"

"You spent a lot of summers here. I just thought you might be sorry to see it go."

"Dad—I haven't been here for years. It's your place, not mine."

"Your mother and I hoped to keep it in the family. You know—a place where you and Jena could come and bring your children, but—"

"I know," Frank interrupted. "No Jena. No kids."

"I just thought I might as well sell it."

"Look—Dad"—Frank was brusque—"why don't we just get going?" He looked around. "What if I drain the hot water tank?"

"It would have been nice," his father said, "to have other kids grow up here."

"I'm going to go drain the hot water tank," Frank said.

His father blinked. "Do you remember how?"

Frank nodded.

"I can show you if you've forgotten."

"Dad, I remember." He spoke like a schoolboy reciting a lesson: "Hose out the window, lower than the level of the heater."

"Don't forget to turn it off when you're done."

"I know, I know."

When Frank came back from the cellar with a hose, his father had gone upstairs. Frank attached one end of the hose to the water heater spigot, uncoiled it across the floor, and dropped the other end out the window. He turned on the spigot; rust-colored water spluttered, then gurgled steadily onto the ground. He wet a sponge and ran it across the sink and stove and table. By the flapping sounds upstairs, he knew his father was covering furniture with sheets and canvas. Frank looked at the grease traps on the stove— clean. He opened the oven. Charred grease rimmed the bottom pan and ridging. *One thing they didn't do,* he thought grimly. He closed the oven door and rechecked the hose. Only a small trickle was now coming out. He uncoupled it from the heater, dragged it across the floor, and dumped it out the window. A cardinal with a missing tail feather immediately landed and hopped along its length, as if inspecting it. Frank turned off the heater, swept the floor, and went upstairs.

In his old bedroom, Frank found his father adjusting a sheet to drape over the chest of drawers. The ship in the bottle that Frank had made one summer still sat on top. *It's amazing someone hasn't stolen it,* he thought. His father picked it up and held it out to him.

"Do you want to take this back with you?" he asked.

Frank shook his head.

"I helped you make this, remember?" his father said. "Remember how you couldn't get the sails to untangle?"

"You keep it, Dad."

"Well—all right. I will." He carefully placed it on the bed and finished draping the sheet over the chest of drawers. "Finished in the kitchen?"

Frank nodded. "I drained the tank and cleaned up a bit."

"How was the oven?"

"Fine," he lied.

"These were really good renters," his father said admiringly. "They usually forget that."

Frank looked out the window. Clouds the color of iodine

were massing at the far end of the lake. "Looks like rain," he said. "But there's not much left to do, I guess."

"Oh, there's a lot to do," his father replied. "We've got to mow the lawn, clean the chimney—"

"You mean cap it, don't you?"

"No—I mean clean it. That's something you can do. I don't like going up on the ladder anymore."

"Dad—you don't need to clean the chimney. Let the new people worry about it."

"It hasn't been cleaned in two years. It should be done."

"Dad, it's a waste of time!"

"Why are you in such a hurry? Where are you going anyway?"

"Well, if you think it's so important, you do it," Frank snapped.

His father worked his lips together the way he did when upset, then walked out the bedroom and down the stairs. The front door slammed.

Frank pounded his fist against the wall. He paced the room, glanced out the window, sat on the bed, then rose and looked again out the window. His father was pushing a wheelbarrow containing bricks, rags, and a burlap bag—materials to make a cleaning bag for the chimney.

Stubborn old man, Frank thought. He pulled up a chair and watched. His father dumped the contents of the wheelbarrow on the ground, then disappeared around the side of the house. In a few minutes he was back, a ladder precariously balanced on his shoulder.

Frank went downstairs and leaned against the porch railing. His father was stuffing the burlap bag with rags and bricks.

"How are you going to carry that up the ladder?" Frank asked.

His father didn't reply.

"Look—do you want me to do it?"

His father nodded toward the hose under the kitchen window. "You didn't put that away."

"You'll need it to soak the cleaning bag," Frank retorted. "Won't you?"

His father looped clothesline rope around the neck of the bag and jerked it tight. "Did you turn off the water heater?" he asked.

Frank slapped his hand against his thigh. "I knew you'd ask! I just knew it. Yes—I turned off the goddamn water heater."

His father dragged the heavy bag to the foot of the ladder. Grasping a side with one hand and holding the bag with the other, he mounted unsteadily.

He'll break his neck, Frank thought.

His father climbed another few rungs, leaning into the ladder for support.

"Dad—come on down," Frank said. "I'll do it."

"No."

Frank went to the foot of the ladder and grasped the bottom of the bag. Above him, his father tugged, but Frank held on. "Dad, come on. I said I'd do it."

"You don't want to."

"I don't want you to break your neck. Please. Just come on down."

"I can do it," his father said, but didn't move. Frank tugged again, and his father climbed down. He dropped the bag at the foot of the ladder.

"I'll just go mow the lawn," he said. When he was out of sight, Frank kicked the bag, hard. Then he sighed, readjusted the ladder and climbed. He pushed the bag onto the roof and went back down for the hose. The cardinal had returned, and was hopping about it. "Beat it," Frank barked. He coupled the hose to the outside spigot and hauled it up. On the other side of the house, the lawn mower sputtered and came to life.

Frank wet down the burlap bag and lowered it down the chimney. When it touched bottom, he raised it, then lowered it again, over and over. When he withdrew it, the bag was black with ash. He hosed it down. Sooty water ran down the roof. He stomped on the bag to squeeze out more soot. Alone on the roof, his arms aching from the weight of the bag, Frank felt his anger trickle away with the dirty water.

His father went by below, more pulled by the lawn mower than pushing it. He'd taken off his chinos and put on old plaid Bermuda shorts with a tear that ran from pocket to leg. His belt slipped from the flesh of his waist, and his thin legs, white and almost hairless, seemed frail. His jaw was thrust forward, intent on the grass ahead of him. A tenderness, warm and unbidden, almost made Frank call to him, to say what he didn't know. The mower spluttered, coughed, and died. His father knelt down and extracted a thick clump of earth and grass from the blades. He turned it over in his fingers, as if it were something rare and marvelous, then tossed it away. He restarted the mower and was gone.

Frank got the chimney cap from the cellar and covered the chimney. With a shout, he threw the burlap bag off the roof. When he reached the ground, he started to untie the bag, then hesitated.

He'll never need this again, he thought. He listened. The lawn mower was on the far side of the house.

Frank dragged the bag to the edge of the dock and heaved it into the lake. It splashed thickly, and sank. Ripples slapped the pilings; the rope swing swayed gently in the breeze. When Frank returned to the house, his father had finished and was putting the mower in the trunk of the car.

"All done?" he asked Frank.

"Yep."

"You put the bag away?"

Frank nodded.

"Well, we're getting to the end now," his father said. "We can do the storm shutters and drain the pipes after lunch."

"Maybe we should just keep going, Dad," Frank suggested. "It looks like rain."

"We've got time. Let's eat."

His father got the cooler from the car. They sat on the porch steps and ate a lunch of tuna fish sandwiches, macaroni salad, sweet pickles, and grapes. Frank opened two beers and handed one to his father. The light had turned leaden, and the clouds that had been massing at the far end of the lake now rolled overhead, imparting a dull sheen to the water. The breeze curled their paper napkins. Frank flicked a ladybug from his knee. He looked at his father. The older man seemed lost in thought, raising sandwich to mouth in slow, careful movements, almost unaware that he was eating. Frank leaned against the porch steps and breathed deeply. The lake smelled old and moldering, like the underside of a decaying log.

"So how are you doing?" his father asked, breaking their silence.

"In what?"

"In everything. Life."

"Okay. I'm getting along."

"You're still living in an apartment?"

"Jena and I sold the house, Dad. You know that."

"And it's okay? This apartment?"

"It's small. An efficiency." Frank laughed. "It's probably not much bigger than my old room here."

"Ah."

"It suits me," Frank said defensively. "I don't need much space."

They lapsed again into silence. Frank folded his napkin, reopened it, and folded it again. His father cleared his throat.

"I just don't know why you never came back," he said.

"What do you mean?"

His father waved to indicate the lake, the house. "All these years, you never once came back here. Right after college— bingo!—you were gone. You could've spent a few weeks here in the summer with your mother and me. But you never did."

"You know how things are," Frank said. "I moved to another state. I married Jena—"

"You could've brought Jena here. You know how much we liked her. We kept inviting the two of you."

Frank pursed his lips.

"We could've all been together," his father said. "It would've made your mother happy."

"Dad—don't make me feel bad about this. There's no reason to." Frank began clearing the remnants of their lunch. He tossed the plastic utensils and paper plates into a grocery bag. "Finished?" he asked, pointing to his father's beer. He nodded, and Frank tossed it into the bag.

"So how is Jena?" his father asked.

"Fine." Frank snapped the lids onto the salad containers. "She's fine."

"What's she doing now?"

"I really don't know."

"Don't you talk to her?"

"Dad"—Frank held out his hands, palms up—"we're divorced. She lives in another state."

"Everybody seems to live in another state," his father murmured.

"It's over with us, Dad. Dead and buried."

"That's what happens with the woman you loved? You declare her dead? You just bury her?"

Frank stood up. "Let's not talk about this anymore, okay?" He walked over to the trash barrel and threw the garbage bag in.

"There won't be another pickup till spring, you know," his father called.

"Jesus!" Frank retrieved the sack, opened the car door, and hurled it into the footwell. He got inside and closed the door. His father called out something else, but it was obscured by a rumble of thunder. Frank rolled up the window. He slammed his palm against the dash. He got out of the car. His father was staring at the lake and didn't look at him when he came up.

"I want to ask you something," Frank said. "You think it's my fault that Jena and me split, don't you?"

"I wouldn't know."

"But you do, don't you?"

His father stood up. "What does it matter? It's over, like you said."

"Well, your darling Jena wasn't so spotless," Frank said. "I could tell you stories about her."

"I'm going to get the storm shutters," his father said.

Frank pursued him across the lawn to the cellar. "You blame me for not giving you any grandchildren, too, don't you?" His father lifted a storm shutter and brushed by him. Frank followed him back outside. "Don't you?"

His father dropped the shutter on the ground. "It would've made your mother happy."

"Well, I'm glad we didn't have kids," Frank said. "I mean, look what happened."

"I don't know why you say that like you're proud," his father snapped. He carried out another shutter and stacked it by the first. Frank began helping, and they worked together in tense silence until all the shutters were outside. The sky was much darker, and a small chop had picked up on the lake. Frank could smell the rain. He picked up one of the storm shutters and began carrying it to the kitchen window.

"Wait!" his father cried. "That's not the right one."

Frank lowered it. "What are you talking about?"

"That one doesn't go to that window. Come here, I'll show you." He pointed to the underside of the shutter: the numeral 5 was marked in grease pencil on the frame. "I've got a system. See—this one goes to window number five."

Frank stared. "What the hell is window number five?"

"I number them starting from the northwest corner, bottom floor, around the house clockwise."

"Dad—what difference does it make? They're all the same size."

His father shook his head. "The shutters can warp differently. For each window."

"Dad, I bet if I took *this* shutter"—Frank pointed—"and put it on *that* window, it would fit just fine. Want to see?"

"What if you got all the way around and found the last one didn't fit? You'd have to redo everything."

"Well, I'll redo everything, then!" Frank said. "By myself. You won't have to do a damn thing."

"No one can tell you anything," his father said.

"Because it's crazy!"

"You know it all."

"No—*you* know it all. *You* can't be told anything."

"Why are you getting so excited?"

Frank threw up his hands. "Okay. We'll do it your way. This is shutter number five, we'll put it on window number five. Or maybe we should start with number one, to really do it right?" He turned over the shutters. "Come on—let's find number one." The heavy frames fell against one another. "I mean, we really want to do this right, don't we?"

"Stop it!"

Frank let a shutter fall. "You don't think I can do anything right, do you? You think I screw up everything. I've screwed up my marriage, I haven't given you any grandchildren, I've got a fourth-rate job—"

"I never said this!"

"Oh, but you think it, don't you? I can't do anything right. Why don't you just admit it?"

"I never—"

"I'm just not perfect like you, am I?"

"I—"

"Do you want to know why I never came back? Do you

really want to know?" Frank's voice was quavering. "Because I couldn't wait to get away from you. You and your nagging and your judging. I just couldn't *wait* to get away!" He sat down heavily on the stack of shutters. "I still can't."

His father blinked. He opened his mouth as if to say something, then turned and walked down the slope toward the lake. The first droplets of rain spattered the ground.

"And now you'll probably blame me for not getting the windows up in time," Frank called after him. "Well, I'll do it anyway! I'll do it your way even." He carried a shutter to the window and hooked it over the window frame. "Number one, we'll just put it right here." Frank jammed it in place. "There!" he cried. He found shutter number two and put it on the corresponding window. "Do it right, do it right, do it right," he muttered as he hit the sides of the shutter to fix it in place. A bolt of lightning crackled over the lake; rain began falling in thick, scattered drops. Frank saw his father on the dock, arms folded, gazing over the water. He picked up another shutter, then hesitated.

"Dad," he called, "it's raining." His father didn't seem to hear.

"Why don't you come on up?" he yelled, but his father didn't move.

All right, stand there, Frank thought. *See if I care.*

Hurrying now to beat the downpour, Frank continued putting the storm shutters on the lower-floor windows. He imagined the interior of the house becoming progressively darker as the shutters cut off the last light that could get inside. *Like it's going to bed,* his mother used to tell him when he was a child, *going to sleep for the winter, and when spring comes, we'll wake it up.* After finishing, Frank returned to the back of the house and looked toward the lake. His father was gone.

"Dad?" he called. Lightning stitched the sky. Frank walked to the water's edge. The breeze gusting off the lake made him shiver. He scanned the cove. "Dad, where are you?"

He heard a rustling in the trees that overarched the water and looked up. His father stood high above on the oak limb by the rope swing. He was breathing heavily from his climb.

"Dad, what the hell are you doing up there!"

"How—high—"

"What?"

"I wanted to see—how high this was."

"What are you talking about?"

"You said it was high. I wanted to see." His father held tight to the rope on the slippery limb.

"So now you've seen," Frank said anxiously. "Come on down before you break your neck."

His father tugged on the rope; the overhead branches made a whisking sound. "It is high," he said. "You were right."

"Dad—"

His father waved as if in salute, then grasped the thick rope with both hands and swung out over the cove, his shirt fluttering behind. Frank opened his mouth, but no sound came out, the only cry his father's as he reached the far point of his arc and let go, the rope falling away as he fell, arms swinging, into the lake. He landed bent over, partly on his stomach. The water churned where he'd entered.

"Dad," Frank murmured in disbelief.

He waited for his father to come up. But he didn't. Nothing moved in the water except the pocking of rain on its surface and the fast-receding ripples from his father's plunge.

"Dad?" Frank called. He went onto the dock and peered

into the rain-flecked water. The lake was dark: he could see nothing below.

"Dad!" he screamed. "Oh Jesus—" Frank ran to the dock's edge. He tore off one shoe and had the other in his hand when his father surfaced with a whoop farther down the cove. He shook his head like a playful seal and began to breast-stroke slowly toward the dock. Frank sat down, his legs dangling over the edge like a helpless marionette's. He seemed to be laughing and crying at the same time, and try as he might, he couldn't stop. His father must have been confused, since he cried out, "What's the matter?" and "What's wrong?" but Frank could only shake his head, and raise his hand, and let it drop.

"I thought you were dead," he said, the words choked, as if it were he that had been drowning. He dropped the other shoe into the water and held out his now empty hands. "I thought you were dead, but you weren't."

Love, Your Only Mother

I received another postcard from you today, Mother, and I see by the blurred postmark that you're in Manning, North Dakota now and that you've dated the card 1961. In your last card you were in Nebraska, and it was 1962; you've lost some time, I see. I was nine years old in 1961. You'd left my father and me only two years before. Four months after leaving, you sent me—always me, never him—your first postcard, of a turnpike in the Midwest, postmarked Enid, Oklahoma. You called me "My little angel" and said that the sunflowers by the side of the road were tall and very pretty. You signed it, as you always have, "Your only mother." My father thought, of course, that you were in Enid, and he called the police there. But we quickly learned that postmarks meant nothing: you were never where you had been, had already passed through in the wanderings only you understand.

A postcard from my mother, I tell my husband, and he grunts.

Well, at least you know she's still alive, he says.

Yes.

This postcard shows a wheat field bending in the wind. The colors are badly printed: the wheat's too red, the sky too blue—except for where it touches the wheat, there becoming aquamarine, as if sky and field could somehow combine to form water. There's a farmhouse in the distance. People must live there, and for a moment I imagine you do, and I could walk through the red wheat field, knock on the door, and find you. It's a game I've always played, imagining you were hiding somewhere in the postcards you've sent. Your scrawled message, as always, is brief: "The beetles are so much larger this year. I know you must be enjoying them. Love, your only mother."

What craziness is it this time? my husband asks. I don't reply.

Instead, I think about your message, measure it against others. In the last postcard seven months ago, you said you'd left something for me in a safety deposit box in Ferndale. The postmark was Nebraska, and there's no Ferndale in Nebraska. In the card before that, you said you were making me a birthday cake that you'd send. Even though I've vowed I'd never do it again, I try to understand what you are telling me.

"Your only mother." I've mulled that signature over and over, wondering what you meant. Are you worried I'd forget *you,* my only mother? In favor of some other? My father, you know, never divorced you. It wouldn't be fair to her, he told me, since she might come back.

Yes, I said.

Or maybe you mean singularity: out of all the mothers I might have had, I have you. You exist for me alone. Distances, you imply, mean nothing. You might come back.

And it's true: somehow, you've always found me. When I was a child, the postcards came to the house, of course; but later, when I went to college, and then to the first of several apartments, and finally to this house of my own, with husband and daughter of my own, they still kept coming. How you did this I don't know, but you did. You pursued me, and no matter how far away, you always found me. In your way, I guess, you've been faithful.

I put this postcard in a box with all the others you've sent over the years—postcards from Sioux City, Jackson Falls, Horseshoe Bend, Truckee, Elm City, Spivey. Then I pull out the same atlas I've had since a child and look up Manning, North Dakota, and yes, there you are, between Dickinson and Killdeer, a blip on the red highway line.

She's in Manning, North Dakota, I tell my husband, just as I used to tell my friends, as if that were explanation enough for your absence. I'd point out where you were in the atlas, and they'd nod.

But in all those postcards, Mother, I imagined you: you were down among the trees in the mountain panorama, or just out of frame on that street in downtown Tupelo, or already through the door to The World's Greatest Reptile Farm. And I was there, too, hoping to find you and say to you, Come back, come back, there's only one street, one door, we didn't mean it, we didn't know, whatever was wrong will be different.

Several times I decided you were dead, even wished you

were dead, but then another postcard would come, with another message to ponder. And I've always read them, even when my husband said not to, even if they've driven me to tears or rage or a blankness when I've no longer cared if you were dead or anyone were dead, including myself. I've been faithful, too, you see. I've always looked up where you were in the atlas, and put your postcards in the box. Sixty-three postcards, four hundred—odd lines of scrawl: our life together.

Why are you standing there like that? my daughter asks me.

I must have been away somewhere, I say. But I'm back.

Yes.

You see, Mother, I always come back. That's the distance that separates us.

But on summer evenings, when the windows are open to the dusk, I sometimes smell cities ... wheat fields ... oceans— strange smells from far away—all the places you've been to that I never will. I smell them as if they weren't pictures on a postcard, but real, as close as my outstretched hand. And sometimes in the middle of the night, I'll sit bolt upright, my husband instantly awake and frightened, asking, What is it? What is it? And I'll say, She's here, she's here, and I am terrified that you are. And he'll say, No, no, she's not, she'll never come back, and he'll hold me until my terror passes. She's not here, he says gently, stroking my hair, she's not—except you are, my strange and only mother: like a buoy in a fog, your voice, dear Mother, seems to come from everywhere.

In the Realm of the Herons

When they arrived at the lake, a man called Nye showed Peter and Megan their cabin and then led them down the stone steps to the water's edge—"to see something special, little girl," he said, winking at Megan. He pointed across the lake to the western shore, already burning with late afternoon sunlight. Giant birds circled the treetops, their wings white against the sky, their necks folded back into graceful S-curves.

"Sea gulls," Megan said.

"Nope," replied Nye. "Those are herons. They roost in the trees all along that shore. They nest here summers, then they go south in the fall." He held up a finger. "Listen, now. You can hear them talking."

They listened. Peter heard a high, plaintive crying.

"They're handsome birds," Nye said, "but they sure make one ugly sound." He wet his lips, as if by tasting the air he could hear them better. "In the old days folks used to hunt

them for their feathers. For ladies' "—he drew out the word—
"*chapeaux*. Now they're protected. Folks still pester them
sometimes, though. Kids mostly."

Peter pointed to a white rowboat bobbing against the dock
piling. "Does that belong to the cabin?" he asked.

"Yep," Nye said. "Oars are in the cellar."

"I might row a bit while we're here. Would you like to do
that, honey?"

His daughter shrugged. When they turned back to the cabin,
Megan stayed behind. "I want to watch awhile," she said.

"Man named Burnham owns your cabin," Nye said as they
walked. "Him and his wife used to come down from Ukiah
every summer. Then she died too"—he glanced at Peter, who
nodded slightly to show it was all right—"and he came one
day, took his tools from the cellar, the clothes from the closets,
and just left the rest. Furniture, TV, toaster, the boat, the
works. 'You rent it for me, Nye,' he told me. 'You won't be
seeing me again.' And I haven't, not for sixteen years." Nye
spat on the ground. "People've been making off with things,
I know. I tell him I should make an inventory, but he always
says don't bother." He studied Peter. "When did your wife
die? You don't mind me asking?"

"Four months ago," Peter said.

Nye shook his head. "Don't know what it's like, not to be
married. I've been married my whole life. One day I was
shooting squirrels and riding bikes and then I was married.
I think I'd miss it."

Yes, Peter thought.

"Hope she didn't suffer."

"She didn't suffer at all," Megan said. Without their hearing, she had come up behind them. "She never knew she died."

"Megan," Peter said.

But she was gone, running up the steps to the cabin.

"She didn't want to come here," Peter explained. "I—I thought a vacation would be good for her...for both of us ...she's just eleven..." His thoughts began eluding him, like smoke in the chilling air.

It was true: Kate hadn't known she was going to die. There had been no reckonings, no good-byes. "Routine and minor," the surgeon termed the operation to remove a nasal polyp which had been troubling her breathing. Peter left her the evening before the surgery, and early the following morning— after he'd packed Megan's school lunch and before he'd even remembered Kate was in the operating room—the hospital called, saying he should come. He was met by a tall, jowled man with large-veined hands who introduced himself as Dr. Debcoe, the deputy administrator of the hospital. His words rushed at Peter: *a terrible thing...almost never happened... one chance in a thousand, in ten thousand...a vascular malformation...nicked...the vicinity of the surgery...significant blood loss...difficult to stanch...transfusions, of course* (here he opened his long ivory hands to show he was hiding nothing)...*her vital signs fell so precipitously...shock...*

Peter was dazed. "You haven't hurt her, have you?" he asked. Debcoe looked at him quizzically, and it was then he realized that Kate was dead.

At the funeral, while Peter cried, Megan sat dry-eyed, nervously crossing and uncrossing her thin legs. When he took her hand, it was so cold it startled him, and they both flinched. During the reception at their house afterward, she disappeared. Peter found her sitting on the floor in the guest bedroom, lights out, curtains drawn against the pale March sunlight.

"I don't want people pawing and crying on me anymore," she said.

"They're only trying to be kind, honey."

"I don't want to be looked at anymore."

"Okay, then," Peter said, "stay up here."

She stood up. "I want to go see Marcie." Marcie was her friend, a small girl with owlish glasses who earlier that day had brought a sympathy card to the house.

"Well, you can't," Peter said. "Not right now."

Megan sighed and sat back down.

Peter cleared his throat. "I want you to know," he told her, "that if there's any—feelings—you've got about Mom's dying—" Megan glanced up—"it's okay to talk about them. You know—get them out."

Megan squirmed, then rested her chin in her hands.

"It's better to get them out," Peter repeated.

She was silent.

"So will you do that?"

"Okay, okay," she exclaimed. "You don't need to say it a hundred times."

But when the door closed for the last time and the final guest had gone, Peter fully expected Kate to come in from the kitchen, slightly breathless from her errands, and tell him she was grateful, it had been a chore, she knew, he had done well in her absence, but now she had come back.

He heard a light thumping and scraping on the floor of the upstairs bedroom, a sound at once familiar, but now strange in the silent house: Megan was playing jacks.

In the weeks that followed, while Peter kept stumbling unexpectedly upon his grief, Megan drew a circle around herself, like the safe zone in a children's game where no pursuers may enter and no prisoners may leave.

"You know, I've never seen you cry," Peter said as they were eating dinner one evening. "Not once since your mother died."

Megan twisted a button on her shirt.

"You've got something in the corner of your mouth," he said. She wiped it off.

"Don't you miss her?" he asked.

"Sure," she said, not looking at him. "Do you think I'm a creep?"

"She's become like a stranger," he said to his sister on the phone.

"What do you mean?"

"Everything's different. She's gotten hard."

"She's grieving, that's all."

"I can't talk to her, I—" His voice caught, and for a moment he couldn't speak.

"Peter?"

"I—I keep expecting Kate to come and explain her to me. Kate did that. I mean, she and Kate—"

"Everybody grieves differently."

"—they were together, somehow, in my mind."

"I know," his sister said. "Give her time."

Silence grew between them. Peter could feel it coming, yet couldn't contain it. It was like trying to keep air in a leaking balloon, or breath in a dying body. In the evening he often found himself outside her closed door, hesitating, hardly breathing, not knowing what he wanted to do or say. Sometimes he would knock and ask her a question whose answer he forgot a moment later; more often, he would just walk away.

He began watching her. Once she was doing gymnastics stretches on the sun deck while he stood behind the kitchen curtains. He held his breath, marveling that she could bend so far without snapping. In midstretch, she stopped, her hair half-fallen across her face. Peter drew back.

"What do you want, Daddy?" she called out.

Peter didn't know.

He dreamed one night he was shaking her, yelling words in a language he didn't understand; even though he was hurting her, she kept grinning at him idiotically. Enraged, he shook harder, and she began to come apart in his hands, leaving him holding torn-off limbs from which ran not blood, but something cold and gray, like porridge.

That's why, he thought. *She wasn't a real child after all.*

Horrified, he dropped her arms, and woke. He walked down the hall to Megan's room. The door was ajar. By the glow of the nite-lite, he saw her, eyes open, staring at him warily. She didn't move or take her eyes from him, and neither of them spoke. Peter closed the door. In the morning, he wasn't sure whether or not he'd dreamed it all, but that didn't matter.

We've got to get out of here, he thought.

And so they'd come to the lake. Imagining they would explore
the lake trails, Peter rented bicycles, but the only day they
did bike, Megan furiously pedaled ahead, complaining that
he was too slow. When he grimly set a faster pace, she said
she was tired and wanted to go back. They drank slushes at
a roadside stand and stared into the icy sludge. As they pedaled back to the cabin, the whirring of their bicycle chains
seemed to Peter the loneliest sound he had ever heard. That
was the last thing they did together: Megan didn't want to
go hiking, and she didn't want to go rowing. Soon she found
Krissa, a girl who was staying at a cabin down the road, and
was gone with her much of the day. The only time Peter was
certain of seeing her was at dinner, where his projected hearty
meals soon devolved into frozen dinners, hot dogs, and grilled
cheeses. After eating, Megan returned to Krissa's cabin; her
friend never came to theirs.

"Why don't you stay home one evening?" Peter asked her.

"Why? There's nothing to do here."

"You could talk to me. I never see you."

"We're together all the time, anyway," she said.

So in the evenings Peter often sat alone on the porch. Wind
bristled the treetops; sometimes a fish leaped and seemed to
hang forever before splashing down. He stared through the
dark pines into a future as black and deep as the lake, at the
end of which was a bare kitchen table where he sat, palms
up, expecting nothing. Across the water, he saw lights in other
cabins where people sat together—eating, talking, planning—then followed the curve of the shoreline around to the
darker regions, where the herons roosted. Often he heard

their crying, and sometimes he thought he could see them, even in the dark, as they circled the trees so closely that their wings might have brushed the branches.

He remembered a Japanese folktale Kate had read to Megan when she was little: in it, a fisherman rescues a gull from a net, only to find that it is actually a beautiful princess transformed by an evil magician. Peter smiled, and imagined Kate had become one of those lovely herons. The image drifted on his thoughts as a boat drifted on water.

He decided one afternoon to row to the end of the lake where the herons were. At the convenience store he bought a six-pack of beer and a pair of denim gloves. "It'll be a hot one today," the clerk advised, so Peter also bought sunburn cream and a long-billed cap that said GONE FISHIN'. He found the oars in the cellar, pitched them in the boat, and gingerly stepped inside. The boat rocked, then steadied as it accepted his weight. He untied the painter and pushed off. A few yards out, he began backrowing.

Peter hadn't rowed for years, and his strokes were choppy. He tried feathering the oars but soon returned to his original stroke. Surprised at how hard he was breathing, he slowed his cadence. After a while, he rested. The sun glared off the water. Except for two fishermen in a distant, hazy boat, the lake was abandoned.

Peter opened a beer and drank deeply, then put the can on the floorboards and continued rowing. His stroke seemed longer now, with more bite and pull. The beer can spilled. Twenty minutes more and he was almost there. His arms and wrists ached; despite the gloves, his palms were chafed. He rubbed his arms and applied more sunburn cream. A gust sent ripples skimming across the lake, and wavelets slapped the side of the boat. Peter scooped up a handful of water. It tasted mossy, sepulchral.

Three herons swooped overhead, startling him. He watched them, and then began rowing toward the point along the shore where they'd disappeared into the trees. Soon he was there, breathing hard, but cleanly. Peter hauled in the oars and allowed himself to drift.

No cabins had been built on this side, and the trees came right to the lake's edge, their roots poking through the loamy soil before plunging into the water. Sunlight scoured the saw grass along the bank. Peter drifted and almost bumped into it before he saw it—the ruin of a small dock, its flooring rotted away. He stuck an oar into the muddy bottom for support and carefully stood up. At first he didn't see the house either: it sat some forty yards from shore, surrounded and sheltered by the tall pines. Peter tied his boat to a log that lay half in the water. By grabbing protruding tree roots, he could scramble up the bank.

The old shingle house, once painted green, had been abandoned for some time. Large sections of tarpaper on the roof had blown away, and one section dipped ominously. Except for several large panes in an upper dormer, most of the windows were surprisingly unbroken. Rows of what had once been a vegetable garden ran along one side; a pie plate still clacked against a wooden stake. A summer chair, its wicker seat fallen out, sat under a tree. Above and around him, herons cried as they flew in and out of their nests.

Peter rattled the front door: it was locked, as were the

windows. He peered inside, but could see little through the grime. In back, he found a porch, its screening in tatters, the hook on the outer door long fallen off. A wringer washer sat in one corner; boxes of empty mason jars, a broken broom, two bald tires, and a pile of rusted bolts littered the floor. A woman's once-yellow bonnet, faded and stiff, lay on one of the boxes. Peter expected the inner porch door to be locked also, but it gave way easily.

He entered a kitchen. An old Amana range and ice chest sat heavily along one wall. Dead insects littered the sink. Peter opened the cupboards: except for a sprung mousetrap, they were empty. The kitchen led to a long hallway in whose center a stairway ascended to the second floor. The rooms off the hallway were littered with beer cans and cigarette butts. Peter winced. He went upstairs.

Those rooms were also empty except for more beer cans, an orange crate containing several moldering volumes of a 1911 *Compton's Picture Encyclopedia,* and a pair of men's work boots, the laces still tied, as if their owner had taken ghostly flight. In the last room stood a bureau, its mirror removed from the frame. Peter opened the drawers: he found a baby mouse skeleton and a bag of sachet, dry and faintly fragrant. He gingerly removed the skeleton and threw it out the window. The scent of the sachet seemed to linger in the room. Peter imagined how the summer house must have looked when freshly painted, its starched curtains billowing, the garden musky with vegetables and flowers.

As he left, Peter unlatched a porch window, and locked the kitchen door.

———

Back at the cabin he found a note from Megan saying that she was staying the night at Krissa's and would return in the morning. He picked up the phone to call her, then dialed Nye instead.

"That's the old Cotter place," Nye said. "Never knew the folks myself. It's been empty for years."

"People have broken into it," Peter said. "I saw beer cans."

"Kids, I expect. They get into foolishness."

"How do you get there by land?" Peter asked.

"Don't really know. That old road is chained off. They don't like folks driving over and pestering the herons."

When Peter awoke the next morning, the idea greeted him like the sun, fully formed and perfect: he would buy the house. He would find out who owned it—surely it still belonged to someone—and buy it. Then he would restore it. He would sand and varnish the floors, straighten the warp of the roof, plaster, and shingle. He would repair the dock, sink new pilings, set in planking. No matter that he knew nothing about construction—he would buy books, Nye would help, he would learn. The garden would come back to life. Peter saw the kitchen dressed in curtains, stocked with food, fragrant with fresh-picked herbs. It would be a place he and Megan could come to in summer and on vacations and holidays. Her room would face the tall pines that almost touched the window; his would be the room of the lady with the sachet. Peter imagined a Megan grown to graceful womanhood bringing her own children to the summer house. He would lift his grandchildren onto his shoulders and show them the nests of the herons.

Impatiently, he awaited Megan's return. He called Krissa's cabin every half hour, but no one answered. He paced the porch. He walked to the dock and looked to the spot on the western shore where the house lay hidden, as if fearful it might vanish. When Megan hadn't come back by lunch, Peter drove over to Krissa's cabin. No one was home. He left a note for Megan to return right away. In midafternoon, she did.

"Where've you been?" he asked sharply. "I thought you were coming back this morning."

"We went to a horse show," Megan replied. "Then we all went out for lunch."

"Well, why didn't you call me?"

She shifted uneasily. "Did I have to?"

"Yes! I was worried."

"I'm sorry," she mumbled.

Easy, Peter told himself. *No sense getting angry. Not today.*

"I want to show you something," he said.

"What?"

"A surprise."

She looked at him warily. "What?"

"Let's go to the dock. We have to row there."

"I don't want to row," she said.

"You don't have to. I'll row. You can just sit there like the Queen of Sheba."

"Daddy, I don't want to go."

"Well, you have to," Peter insisted. "It's important. Please."

Megan sighed, but followed him to the boat. Peter pushed them off and jumped in; Megan gripped the gunwales as the boat rocked, then steadied. She sat, chin in hand, staring off the side as Peter rowed. Waterflies danced in anticipation of evening, and once a bass leaped so near that Megan jumped.

Somewhere steaks were frying. It was an afternoon you could
sing to, Peter thought. His daughter trailed her hand over the
side, her fingers delicately lacing the water. Peter searched
her face for traces of Kate, yet could find none: her cheeks,
once they lost their baby fat, would betray his bones.

"This is the life, huh?" he said as he dipped the oars.

Megan was silent.

Peter hesitated, then said, "I wish your mother were here."

"Kate," Megan said. "Her name was Kate."

Peter pulled the oars deeper.

"Do you miss her?" he asked.

"Why do you keep asking me that?"

"Because you never say anything about her! It's as if
she's—"

"She is dead," Megan said. "She died."

"Just answer me—do you miss her?"

"Okay, okay, I miss her! Is that what I'm supposed to say?"

Peter rowed harder, and the boat surged.

"You hate me, don't you?" he said.

She shook her head.

"I didn't kill her, you know."

Megan leaned over the side and began humming.

"Stop that!" he snapped.

She continued humming, louder now.

"Stop it! Look at me."

"What do you want?" she cried. Her face was contorted
in rage. "Why are you always bothering me? Why can't you
just leave me alone?"

Peter stopped rowing. "Look—"

She began humming again.

He dropped the oars. "You know, I'm tired of you," he

said. "I'm sick and tired of you. I'll leave you alone, all right. Maybe you'd like me dead too. Wouldn't you?" She was shaking her head back and forth. "You could really be alone then, right? You little snot!"

"Don't call me names!"

"I'll call you any damn thing I please! I'm your father."

She covered her ears. "Don't yell, don't yell."

"I'll yell all I want!"

"I want to go home," Megan pleaded.

"Well, we're not. We're going where I want to go." Peter picked up the oars and rowed a few fierce strokes, then shoved them over to her. "Here, you row!"

"No!"

"Yes, damn you, you row!"

He grabbed her hands to force the oars into them. "No, no, no," she screamed, clenching her fists. She kicked him. Enraged, he slapped her, then roughly pried open her fingers and closed them around the oars.

"Now—row!" he hissed.

Her chest was heaving, but she wouldn't cry, and she wouldn't row. Peter looked at his daughter across the abyss of the boat. The oars were monstrous in her small hands.

What am I doing? he thought, and was ashamed.

"Here, give them back to me," he said wearily. Megan slumped into her seat, arms tightly folded. Across the lake, a motorboat faded into the wake of its own sound. Peter rowed in silence. When they reached shore, he tied the boat to the log, then helped her up the bank. Megan walked ahead of him, fast, then stopped when she reached the clearing.

"It's just an old house," she said.

No, it's not, Peter thought. But he knew there was nothing he could say about it that she might understand. They would never live here. It had been a madness to think so.

"Why did we come here?" Megan asked.

"I found it yesterday," Peter said. "I—I thought you'd like to see it, that's all."

She wrinkled her nose.

"Let's go around back. We can get in there."

The door that he'd locked the day before was ajar. Someone had been there. Peter pushed it open. "Hello?" he called. The house smelled acrid, coppery, silent.

"Well, let's take a look around." He went into the kitchen, but Megan remained on the porch. "Come on," he urged.

She hesitated, then stepped cautiously into the kitchen.

"Go on," he said. "Look around."

She went down the hall. "Don't follow me," she said.

"Take a look upstairs," he called after her. "There's a box of old encyclopedias there."

Megan glanced in the side rooms, then went upstairs. Peter listened to the groaning boards as she walked through one room, then another. For one moment more, he imagined the house filled with the scent of wood shavings, varnish, paint. He sneezed, and sneezed again. A pollen was in the air, or dust.

Megan was screaming. Peter ran to the stairwell and almost collided with her as she stumbled down. "Megan—" he cried, but she pushed him away, sliding through his hands like water. He looked up the stairwell. "Who's there?" he yelled. "Who are you?" He hesitated, then went up. From her footsteps, he knew in which room she'd been.

For a moment he thought it was standing there, wings and feet outstretched, miraculously risen as no bird ever could, even as he noted the limp head, the glassed and vacant eye. The heron was dead. Nailed against the wall, it was at once enormous and awkward, and in the gracelessness of death, only pitiful. Its eye held Peter. A breeze through the broken window ruffled its feathers. Peter closed the door and left.

He found Megan sitting in the boat, arms wrapped tightly around her knees. Her breathing was harsh, hurried, and when she saw him, she stiffened and held up her hand to come no closer. He sat on the log across from her.

"I didn't know it was there," he said. "It wasn't there yesterday."

She stared at him, the ghost of hate and anger in her eyes. Something in her seemed to quiver, and then she was crying, shaking her head as if to deny it. Peter didn't know what to do or say. He waited, silence at last seeming wise.

"Who would do that?" she moaned. "Who would want to kill it like that?"

"Kids," he said. "I don't know."

"But there's just no reason for it," she sobbed.

Peter thought for a moment. "No," he said. "No reason at all."

It seemed to calm her. Gradually she grew quiet, and lay her head on her arms. "Why did we come here?" she asked.

"I was thinking about buying it. The house." Megan looked up at him. He grinned. "Bad idea, huh?"

She nodded, and again rested her head on her arms, as if she would sleep. The boat gently bumped against the log. "Megan—" he murmured. He wanted her to raise her head; he wanted to see her face, as if she might vanish.

A cool breeze, sharp as rain, blew across the lake. Peter shivered.

"It's just that I don't know where she went," Megan said, and for a moment Peter didn't know who she meant. "She's got to be somewhere, doesn't she? She can't just be nowhere." Megan clasped her arms around her shoulders and lightly rocked. "Sometimes I—I think I could just—you know—just call her up and say, well, okay, let's go out for a Coke. And she'd come. She'd have to come. I'd tell her, It's just not fair, you at least owe me a Coke."

They sat awhile longer, then pushed off. The ripples that had run toward the shore now seemed to run from it, Peter thought. Or was that his imagination? Did lakes have tides? Could they be charted? He pulled the oars deeply through the water: he wanted them back before dusk.

"I'm cold," Megan said.

Peter had nothing to give her. Instead, he began singing. First he sang "The Skye Boat Song," then "Clementine," Megan looking at him with an old look of scorn and embarrassment, but he would not be silenced now. He grinned at her and kept singing, back to the wind, rowing them across water and time to a place that—for lack of any better word—they would have to call home.

Elisabetta, Carlotta, Catherine (Raising the Demon)

"Well, look at this," her husband says to Elisabetta. And hands her a Polaroid photograph, slightly gummy to the touch. They've been sorting through her father's effects in the tiny Florida apartment in which he lived the last fourteen years of his life; dead of an unexpected heart attack at fifty-three, he was buried only yesterday, and she and Mark have come from California for the funeral. Her mother, who also lives in California, but farther south, refused to attend. Viewing him in the casket was the first time Elisabetta had seen him in eighteen years, since she was a little girl. She was amazed by how much he still looked like the father she remembered, the father in those few photographs she's kept from her childhood.

In this photo he looks vigorous, tanned, and happy. He wears cut-off denim shorts and a madras shirt open to the waist. One muscular arm is draped around the thin shoulders of a black woman in a pink-and-blue-striped beach dress: she looks at the camera shyly, reluctantly, unsure of this moment's capture. A little girl of seven or eight, her skin the color of dark honey, holds on to his leg. She has none of her mother's self-consciousness; her lips are pursed, as if she's trying to suppress a grin. Elisabetta's father holds her gently to him. They all look as if they've been to the beach.

In the background stands a two-story white building in the Georgian style. Columns enclose a deep porch; a veranda runs around the perimeter; palms and other blurred foliage surround it. An equatorial languor shimmers in the frame. Elisabetta turns the photo over. In her father's writing, familiar to her from birthday and Christmas cards, is an inscription slightly blurred by the porous paper: *Catherine and Carlotta, Barbados, 1984.* Only a few years ago.

"Who are they?" Mark asks.

Elisabetta shakes her head.

"Maybe your father had a secret life." He looks at the photograph over her shoulder. "She's a beautiful little girl."

"That's funny," Elisabetta says. "That's what he used to call me. His beautiful little girl." She touches the child's face and sees her own staring back from those other photographs, where her father holds Elisabetta much the same way.

She hadn't been much older than this little girl when he left, not exactly abandoning her and her mother, since he regularly sent money, but never returning to them either. Her parents never did divorce, but as far as Elisabetta knows, they also never saw each other again. Her father wandered to other cities and other states, finally settling in Florida. At first he called occasionally, and her mother would speak to him in a tense voice behind the kitchen door. Sometimes she called

Elisabetta in, and handed her the phone, and her father's voice would cheerily ask how she was, had she grown any, how was school. Out of fear of embarrassing them both, Elisabetta never asked what she most wanted to know—if he was coming back. In time, the phone calls stopped, replaced by short, sporadic letters which over the years were replaced by even shorter notes, accompanied by small checks, on Christmas and birthday cards. Elisabetta decided she didn't care if he returned. In junior high she told her friends that he was dead. In college she resurrected him, telling herself that he was probably tormented by guilt and sorrow, and that's why he'd remained so distant. *I can almost feel sorry for him,* she decided generously.

"I just don't understand how a father wouldn't want to see his daughter," Mark had said when they were dating.

Elisabetta shrugged.

"Haven't you wanted to see him?"

"Sometimes," she said.

"Why haven't you?"

"I don't know. It might be terrible." She laughed. "Besides, what if he thought I wasn't so pretty anymore?"

She didn't invite him to their wedding. Instead, she sent an announcement, writing on it, "I'm someone else's little girl now." Immediately after sending it she felt ashamed, and almost wrote him, but didn't. He sent her a card with a short note of congratulations and a check, which she never cashed.

When he died, Elisabetta felt a relief—that he was gone at last, and with his going the knowledge that, after all, he *had* been there, as close as a telephone or an airplane trip, yet as far away as the moon. It no longer mattered, she told herself, what he felt about her, or she about him: he was gone, and so was the necessity of choosing between love and hate. What had begun years ago had ended.

Now she looks at this photograph in which her father and another little girl are smiling at her.

"That's his child," she says to Mark.

"Why? Why assume that?"

"For the same reason her name's Carlotta and mine's Elisabetta. He liked Italian names."

"Maybe it's the other way around. Maybe the woman's Carlotta."

"No," she says, "that wouldn't be right." She stares at the photograph. "They probably don't even know he's dead."

Mark flies back to California the next day, but Elisabetta stays on for a while to settle her father's affairs. She can find no records, no letters, nothing that can help identify Carlotta and Catherine. She often takes out the photograph and studies each face in turn, as if one might speak to her.

My father's other family, she thinks. *My other mother. My dark sister.*

She fears the photo is becoming soiled with handling. She polishes it with a soft cloth, then worries that she's scratched it.

"I'm going to Barbados," she tells Mark over the phone. "I want to find them."

He's stunned. "Elisabetta—why?"

"They don't know he's dead. They'll think he abandoned them."

"What makes you think he didn't?"

"He loves her—the little girl. I can tell."

"Elisabetta, they're not your concern!"

"I want to talk with them," she says.

"About what?"

"Him. I want to know what he was like to them."

"Elisabetta, this is crazy."

"I deserve to know," Elisabetta says. "He was my father before he was hers."

"Then wait'll I get some vacation time. We'll both go."

"No. I want to go now." She presses her fingers against her cheek, and the pressure of nails against her skin is somehow comforting.

Mark sighs. "Just how do you think you'll find them?"

"I've looked at a map. Barbados is a small island. I'll find that building in the picture. Somebody there will remember him. Or know them. It wasn't that long ago."

After her plane lands in Bridgetown, the tall customs officer in sunglasses stamps Elisabetta's passport with hardly a glance. She shows him the photograph and asks if he recognizes the building. His eyes flicker behind the purplish lenses.

"Ask the taxi boys," he says, pointing to the cellophaned exit doors.

As soon as she steps outside, they swarm about her, each importuning her to ride with him. The wind blows up dust from the pavement, stinging her eyes, and she has the impulse to flail at them. She puts her bag down, and when she opens her eyes, it's in the hands of a portly driver with a face like a licorice moon.

"King Creole, mum," he says, smiling. "Easy to remember. Like the movie by Elvis. Taxi?"

The other drivers good-naturedly fall away. Elisabetta follows him to an old Chevrolet whose paint is peeling in thick, rusty flakes. A sign on the door, carefully cleaned, announces KING CREOLE'S ISLAND TAXI TOURS. TOP SIGHTS, BOTTOM PRICE. And almost as an afterthought: SPECIAL EVENTS ARRANGED. He tosses her bag in the front seat. Inside, it smells of burnt plastic and sweat. A gummy photograph on the dash identifies the driver as Stanley Augustus Tremaine.

"Where to, mum?" he asks.

Elisabetta hasn't booked any reservations. "A hotel," she says.

He turns and looks at her. "Any particular one, you say?"

She is tired and can't think. "No. Yes—wait." Elisabetta extracts the photograph from her purse. "Is this a hotel? I mean—do you recognize it?"

He studies the photograph, then breaks into a grin.

"I do believe—I would swear to—that this"—he taps the photo with a thick finger—"be the Lime House, before they repaint. Up by Vierge's Hill. Very nice place. Posh, but not too. Quiet. Private beach, of course. First class all the way."

How easy, Elisabetta thinks. *How very easy.*

They are soon on a narrow country road. Sugarcane lines the route; in the distance, a squall is moving down the side of a blue-green mountain, small and thick as a thumb. They pass flimsy wooden houses that tilt at odd angles and equally flimsy corrugated tin buildings which advertise bicycle repair, soft drinks, canned goods. Everything seems as if it is either rusting or becoming green before her eyes. The wind rushes through the window and blows Elisabetta's hair. She smells hot tar bubbling up from the road and some other smell, dusky and sweet, promising night.

"Are you really King Creole?" she asks.

"Yes, mum."

"And you're Stanley Augustus Tremaine also," she reads.

He laughs. "Him too, mum."

Elisabetta hands her photo back to him. "Do you recognize any of these people?"

He takes it in one hand, while with the other he swerves to avoid two boys on bicycles who carry a large fish between them. "Crazy, you!" he shouts out the window. The taller boy grins and waves. Elisabetta can smell the pungent fish as they pass. Stanley looks at the photo.

"Him, no. Not the woman neither," he says amiably. "Friends?"

"My father."

"Ah."

"And friends of his," she adds. "I've—I've come to find them."

"What fun," Stanley says, beaming.

They climb a hill and pull into a semicircular driveway before a lime-colored building that sits among the shadows of palms, banana trees, hibiscus, and azalea. An iron balustrade, intricately worked with floral motifs, runs along the veranda; the shutters of the tall French windows repeat the curve of the drive. Several outbuildings—guest cottages, Elisabetta supposes—stand half-hidden in the foliage. A gardener is trimming hedges while another spreads potash around the base of a banana tree. As Stanley unloads her bag, Elisabetta studies the Lime House: something seems wrong.

"It's not like the photo," she says.

Stanley smiles. "They paint it last season. Make it green like the lime."

"No—I mean, it's different. It's the same, but it's not."

He looks again at the photograph. "Other side, mum. Beach side. There it'll be."

The beach, Elisabetta thinks. *Of course.*

"I do tours for guests here," Stanley tells her as the bellboy comes up. "All the island, all top sights. Maybe for you? For such a pretty lady I'd give best price. No? Well, I'm here by and by. Ask for the King." He winks, tips his hat, drives off. Elisabetta follows the bellboy inside.

"Luckily, it is off-season," the clerk at the reception desk informs her. "During high season, we're fully booked." He is pleased to have such good news. He picks up what looks like a Halloween ratchet and twirls it. Another bellboy silently appears and conducts Elisabetta to a room on the second floor. He puts her bag on the bed and opens the French windows to sunlight and the afternoon breeze. The curtains billow. He opens the door to the bath, turns on the light, accepts his tip, and leaves without saying a word.

Elisabetta eagerly looks out the window: a closely cropped lawn dotted with croquet wickets stretches down to the beach. Two gardeners with power mowers are making opposing sweeps on either end of the lawn. Elisabetta hears the *thock* of tennis balls from courts hidden by trees; to her right, she sees a small English garden with white chairs, a stone walkway, a miniature windmill, a pond.

She is here, where he was, where they were.

Elisabetta puts on a fresh skirt and blouse, takes her camera, and goes down to the lawn. She doesn't look back until she imagines she's at the appropriate point, then turns: she's now standing in the same spot as the unknown photographer who took the picture of her father, Carlotta, and Catherine. She takes that photograph from her skirt pocket and holds it close to her eyes, superimposing it over the real hotel. She lowers it, and can almost see them all standing there still, like a shimmering after-image. A small terrier runs up the lawn while a middle-aged couple dressed in matching yellow polo shirts and Bermuda shorts walks toward her. The man carries a plastic shopping bag; his wife leans on his arm. Elisabetta snaps a picture of the Lime House. The man and woman smile reflexively.

"We're the Ralstons," the woman says to her. She grasps Elisabetta's arm. "We're from Connecticut and we're having a fine time. Did you just come?"

"Yes," Elisabetta replies.

"Well, you'll have a fine time, too. It's like a second honeymoon for us."

They watch the picture develop in Elisabetta's hand. The two photographs are almost identical: in one stand her father, Carlotta, and Catherine; in the other, the Ralstons and the small dog who flees the frame. The flowers, the bushes, the arching palms—all seem the same, as if preserved in a tropical bell jar for Elisabetta's coming.

"This is my father, and some friends of his," she tells them. "I'm here looking for them."

"How nice," Mr. Ralston says. "Are they lost?"

"Yes. I mean, no—I've just got to find them."

Ralston twirls the bag in his hand, and something clacks.

"Don't do that, you'll break them," his wife admonishes. "Seashells," she tells Elisabetta. "That's all he does here—look for seashells."

"It's a good beach for them," he says. He winks at her.

"He pays no attention to me," Mrs. Ralston says. "But I'm patient with him." She smiles, revealing teeth stained around the gumline. She studies the photograph once again. "Such a cute little girl," she says of Carlotta. "She's like a picture herself."

But no one at the Lime House has any memory of her father, nor of Catherine and Carlotta—not the bell captain, who each evening solemnly hands Elisabetta the menu; nor the waiters who hover just out of sight, reappearing to fill her water glass before it's even half empty; nor any of the bellboys who call to each other in patois across the lobby and lawn. The front desk has no record of her father's ever having been a guest.

"But they *did* stay here." Elisabetta points to the photograph. "Just look."

"Maybe they come just for the day, mum," the assistant manager tells her.

"Why would they come way out here? And besides, isn't this a private beach?"

He smiles and shrugs. "Why would you be wanting to find them, mum?"

"I want to talk with them. I—I have a message for them. From him."

Again, a smile. "Why not try the authorities, mum? It's more their sort of work, isn't it?"

She takes the hotel minivan to Bridgetown and goes to the constabulary.

"Why would you be looking for them, miss?" the young constable also asks. The way he's holding the photograph, Elisabetta is worried he'll smudge it.

"My father—there—has died. These were friends of his.

I think they live here, on Barbados. I want to give them some money he left them." Perhaps the mention of money will help; perhaps just the lie will.

The constable taps his nose reflectively. "I'm afraid we can't help, miss. These are private matters. Not police work at all."

"Isn't there anything you can do?"

He props the photo against a book and studies it. "I could post this in the duty room, I suppose."

"It's my only copy," Elisabetta says. "I don't want to leave it. Maybe I could get another made somewhere?"

He yawns. "There's a chemist three streets over."

She follows his directions but can't find the chemist. She asks two teenage girls who are sitting on the sidewalk listening to island music on a cassette player; they laugh and shake their heads. The smell of tar and rotting vegetables is everywhere. Elisabetta's dress clings to her skin, and she feels flushed. She realizes that she doesn't want to leave her photograph with anyone at all; what she wants to do most now is to sleep. When she finds herself back in the square by the wharves, she hires a taxi to the Lime House. Along the way they pass a line of schoolgirls in starched blue-and-white uniforms, all carrying identical leather satchels. Elisabetta searches their faces, but the taxi speeds by too fast, and the schoolgirls vanish behind her.

She could have been there, Elisabetta thinks. *It is so easy to miss someone.*

She walks the lawn and walks the beach and imagines them here. A man carrying a little girl on his back runs into the surf. He makes animal sounds and the little girl screams with delight. The man scoops her through the waves so that the water skims through the top of her swimsuit. Then he makes chugging sounds, like an engine. The little girl thrashes ecstatically.

That could have been Carlotta, Elisabetta thinks. *It could have been me.*

Someone is calling her. She shades her eyes and looks around. It is Mrs. Ralston. Her husband is farther off, walking by the waterline, eyes downcast.

"I said, 'Are you having any luck finding your father?'" For some reason Mrs. Ralston thinks that it's he Elisabetta is searching for, not Carlotta and Catherine. Elisabetta doesn't feel like correcting her.

"No," she replies. "No luck at all."

Mrs. Ralston points to her husband. "Look at him. He won't leave this beach. He doesn't even like shells, you know." They watch Ralston bend over and pick one up. He washes the shell in the surf, studies it, casts it away. "It was my idea to come on this vacation, and now he's ignoring me."

Ralston sees them and waves.

"He likes you, you know," Mrs. Ralston tells her. "He thinks you're quite lovely."

"Everyone does," Elisabetta says without thinking. She's shocked she's said this. "I'm sorry, I didn't mean it the way it sounded."

"But you *are* a lovely girl." Mrs. Ralston lightly touches her arm, and Elisabetta flinches. "Your husband is very lucky."

Seeing the schoolchildren has given Elisabetta an idea: she will visit schools in the area and show her photograph. She doesn't know why she didn't think of it sooner. After trying to find Stanley Augustus Tremaine, who's not available, she hires another taxi. Her driver is a thin man with badly pocked yellow-brown skin; he is completely silent as they drive, which both suits Elisabetta and makes her uneasy. The front desk has provided the addresses of several lower schools. "Still being the detective, mum?" the clerk asked, amused.

"Yes," Elisabetta said. "All the time."

At the first school—a small whitewashed building that smells of mildew and soggy paper—she talks to the assistant headmaster. He is a tall, ascetic-looking young man who never quite looks her in the eye. He sits formally behind his desk and presses together the tips of his fingers. Elisabetta hands him the photograph, and he immediately places it on his desktop, as if it's too delicate to touch.

"Why would you be interested in finding this girl?"

Elisabetta is used to the question by now. "My father— there—died. He left them some money."

"Ah." He picks up the photo and tips it to the light. The small electric fan on his desk turns in its cycle and blows on Elisabetta; she feels the hair on her arm tingle. He studies the photo for a long time, then hands it back, shaking his head solemnly.

"I'm sorry. She's not with us." He says it without looking at her.

At the next school a woman in the headmaster's office is typing, letter by exacting letter, on an old machine. "If you have no appointment," she tells Elisabetta, "then you must wait." Elisabetta sits in a hard-backed chair, and the woman resumes her pained typing. The sound of the keys hitting the soft paper becomes oppressive in the morning heat and Elisabetta wishes the woman would finish, but she types on and on.

"Excuse me," Elisabetta says after ten minutes have passed. The woman looks at her with irritation.

"The headmaster? Is he in a meeting?"

The woman shakes her head. "I told you. You must wait."

"Well, can you at least tell him I'm here?"

"He is not here."

"Why didn't you tell me that?"

The woman shrugs.

"When will he be back?"

The woman shrugs again. "Later."

Elisabetta takes a deep breath, and rises. "I'll come back later, then." She must get out of this room. But at the door she hesitates, then goes over to the woman's desk. "Maybe you can help me," she says, and shows her the photograph. "Do you know—is this child—in your school?"

The woman glances suspiciously at the picture. "You'll have to ask the head," she says. "I surely can't answer that."

The third school, much larger than the others, is surrounded by an iron paling. Children are playing in the courtyard. Elisabetta walks over to the paling and scans their faces as best she can, but sees no one who resembles Carlotta. A little girl standing on the other side watches her shyly.

Elisabetta smiles at her. "Hello."

The girl averts her eyes.

"You're very pretty," Elisabetta says. The little girl now smiles, but still won't look at her.

"Can you come here? I want to show you something." The girl hesitates, then approaches. "Do you know this little girl?" Elisabetta passes her the photograph through the bars. The girl looks at it and shakes her head. Elisabetta smiles gamely. "All right—thank you." She holds out her hand for the photograph, but the little girl doesn't hand it back.

"My picture," Elisabetta says. "Can I have it back, please?" The little girl smiles at her.

"Give me the photo." The girl backs away from the paling.

"Give it to me!" Elisabetta cries. Still smiling, the girl puts the photograph into the pocket of her jumper.

"It's mine!" Elisabetta grasps the bars. "Give it to me, it's mine!" Other children are looking at her now, and she feels she's about to cry.

Someone behind her says something sharply in patois. It's her taxi driver. The little girl stops smiling and comes over to the paling. She passes him the photograph, and he hands it back to Elisabetta.

"Thank you," she says. He nods. She feels that she's looked foolish, and is embarrassed. "I want to go back," she says. As they drive away from the school, the children are going inside, and Elisabetta can no longer see the little girl.

Back in her room at the Lime House, she turns on the fan against the muggy air and puts the photograph into the drawer of the vanity.

The Ralstons invite her over to their table for dinner. The steel band is playing "Jamaica Farewell," one of the four or five songs they repeat endlessly. Mrs. Ralston hums along. She seems nervous, and complains about the heat.

"It's doing terrible things to my hair," she tells them. "It's drying and falling out. A patch came out just this evening. I'm going to be bald."

"If you don't like heat, why come where it's hot?" Ralston

asks. He winks at Elisabetta. "'Down de way/Where de nights are gay,'" he sings.

"I'm beginning to hate that song," Mrs. Ralston says. "It's all I can do not to scream."

"Maybe you should," her husband says. She opens her mouth wide, neck muscles taut, miming a scream. Elisabetta is startled, but then Mrs. Ralston laughs. The steel band segues to "Yellow Bird."

"Oh, I hate it, I hate it," Mrs. Ralston says.

"Let's dance," Ralston says to Elisabetta.

"You can't dance to this," his wife objects.

"Oh, sure you can." He snaps his fingers to the beat.

"I don't know," Elisabetta says.

"Oh, go ahead, satisfy him," Mrs. Ralston urges her.

They try a simple box-step, but the rhythms are wrong. "I can't lead to this," Ralston laughs. He holds her lightly. A fine sheen of perspiration has formed on his forehead. "Are you having a good time?"

"Oh, yes."

"I mean on your vacation. You always look so solemn."

"Do I?"

"No luck with your father?"

"My father's dead."

"Oh—I'm sorry." He's confused.

"I never made it clear, I guess. It's the others I'm looking for."

"I see."

"But I'm not sure I'll find them." This is the first time she's said this, even to herself.

Ralston holds her hand as they walk back to the table. His wife applauds them, smiling tightly.

"Elisabetta's father is dead, you know," Ralston tells her.

"Oh, really?" She's still smiling, as if it's a mask she can't remove. "Well, who will take care of her then?"

When Ralston goes to the bar to freshen their drinks, she grasps Elisabetta's arm. "He's going to leave me," she says.

"What do you mean?"

"I know all the signs. He stops talking to me. He just stares into space, or looks out windows. And then one day he's gone. I don't know where he goes. He never tells. He's always come back, but I'm never sure." Her eyes are wide, distraught. "He knows how much this hurts me. Even here, on our vacation, he wants to get away from me. Do you know what I'm saying?"

Elisabetta shakes her head, then nods. She is frightened of this woman.

"The last time he came back, I wanted him to die. I thought about killing him as he slept. But I didn't. I'm afraid to be without him. I'm weak that way, I'll admit. I'm afraid I'll shrivel up and blow away."

"Maybe he's not going to leave," Elisabetta says.

Mrs. Ralston stares at her. "What do you know? You're a child, an innocent." She glances over at her husband, who's laughing with the bartender. "Sometimes I think about locking him in a room. Only I would have the key. He could dream of leaving all he wants, but that's all it would be." Her eyes glisten, and her grip on Elisabetta's arm tightens painfully. "I want to know everything he's thinking. Is that so wrong? Isn't that what marriage is—the union of two souls?"

"I don't know," Elisabetta says. "My arm—" Mrs. Ralston

looks down at her hand, then slowly uncurls her fingers, as if reluctant to let Elisabetta go.

After dinner she finds a message at the desk that Mark has called. Elisabetta goes to the lobby phone and begins to dial their number, then hesitates. She doesn't want to answer his questions tonight. *I'll call in the morning,* she thinks. Instead, she decides to go for a walk along the road in front of the hotel.

Soft brown eyes watch her from porches and windows as the dusk deepens. A man's high-pitched voice calls to her, and others laugh, but she can't see them. Doves are cooing in the grass, and all at once, as if on signal, frogs begin to croak.

Carlotta, she whispers. *Catherine.* They could be this near.

A woman in a shapeless cotton smock throws a bucket of suds on her steps and begins sweeping. The broom rasps in the musky air. Elisabetta nods as she passes, and the woman nods back.

She, she will know, Elisabetta thinks. But she's left the photograph back in the room, and by the time she returns with it, the woman will be gone.

An old man with bundles of pots and pans tied to his back jangles by. He smiles at Elisabetta; he has no teeth. He says something she can't understand. "What?" she asks, and he repeats, but she still can't understand, and shakes her head helplessly. The old man laughs, waves his hand to show it's all right, and hobbles on.

I will never find them, Elisabetta thinks.

Back in her room, she sits in front of the vanity mirror and takes the photograph from the drawer. She looks at Carlotta's face, then her own, and imagines she can see through the mirror to the porch of a small house where she and Carlotta are sitting. Elisabetta recognizes the house—it's the one she and her mother and father lived in when she was small. Even now her mother and Catherine are inside, laughing, doing all that mothers do indoors on summer evenings. Her father—their father—isn't there yet, but he will come, he will come. Elisabetta and Carlotta hold hands and breathe the sweet, moist air.

Elisabetta, where is he? Carlotta asks.

He'll be here soon, Carlotta.

But how do you know?

He loves you. She strokes the little girl's hair, so much coarser than her own. *You're his beautiful little girl.* They hold hands while fireflies bob up and down in the darkness.

If I was so beautiful, Carlotta says, *then why did he leave?*

"Carlotta—" Elisabetta murmurs. "It wasn't your fault, Carlotta." But she is gone. Elisabetta looks at the photograph. Her father's smile seems to mock her. She takes her fingernail file from its case and holds it, point down, over his face, as if to scratch it. Her fingers tremble. She lowers the file, and quickly puts the photograph back into her purse.

She spends most of the next morning wandering along the beach and through the gardens. She feels adrift, as lost as Carlotta and Catherine. It's early afternoon before she remembers that she hasn't returned Mark's call. By late afternoon, she still hasn't: somehow, it seems too difficult to do.

The Ralstons wave her over at dinner. "We're going to a voodoo party tonight," Mrs. Ralston announces.

"It's not a *party*," her husband corrects her. "These things aren't parties."

"I thought voodoo was just in Haiti," Elisabetta says.

"It's not voodoo either. That King Creole fellow arranged it. One of his 'specials' for the tourists."

"I think it's exciting," Mrs. Ralston says, "whatever it is."

"There he is now." Ralston whistles. Through the open terrace doors, Elisabetta sees Stanley Tremaine waiting by the front desk. Ralston waves him over. The portly taxi driver tips his hat to them all.

"Tell us again just what it is we're going to this evening," Ralston commands.

"The raising of the demon in Bathsheba Grove," Stanley replies.

"A demon?" Elisabetta asks.

Stanley nods. "Living in the Grove. As long as folks there raise him regular, let him know who's boss, he don't do no harm."

"And how do they raise this demon?" Ralston asks.

"They make a big fire and call him. Demon comes to the fire. Demons always be cold—always looking for the hot."

"What happens if they don't raise him?" Elisabetta asks.

"He do all kinds of mischief. Knots in mules' tails. Women having sour times. Making things disappear that you treasure up."

"Doesn't sound so terrible to me," Ralston snorts.

"But here's the best," Stanley says. "When he gets raised proper, and he's in the fire, you can ask him what your heart desires and he'll tell you. You've got to give him something though. Something you hold true and precious."

"Like what?" Mrs. Ralston asks.

Stanley shrugs. "The demon knows. You give it to him in the fire. If he knows it's precious to you, he answers. If not, then he don't." He looks at Elisabetta. "You come too, pretty lady. Ask the demon 'bout those you seek."

"Yes, why don't you come?" Mrs. Ralston says brightly. She leans closer. "I'm afraid I'll be the only white woman there," she whispers, still smiling. "Please say you'll come."

They leave in Stanley's taxi, the only three from the hotel going to the demon-raising. Mrs. Ralston grips her husband's arm; he smells of a new bay-rum cologne he has bought. He hums a tune and stares out the window. Moon-flecked clouds float by Mount Hillaby, which turns gray, then slate blue as they drive past endless fields of cane. Frogs are everywhere. The darkening air is as thick and sweet as syrup.

Stanley turns straight into a cane field; there is a small dirt path, barely big enough for the taxi. The cane on either side reaches through their open windows. Then they are in a clearing, the cane cut back some fifty yards from a gnarled toyon tree left standing in the field. Packing boxes are piled near the tree, and empty rum bottles glint in Stanley's headlights.

"This is Bathsheba Grove?" Ralston asks.

Stanley waves his hand. "Over there. Through the cane. But this be where the demon lives."

Elisabetta and the Ralstons are the only tourists there, aside from two young men—German, perhaps—who have identical blond mustaches and close-cropped blond hair. They wear shorts and running shoes and carry cameras around their necks. An old man is having difficulty lighting a fire with wood stripped from packing crates. He calls out in a series of high-pitched cries, and a young man who has been talking with two women brings over a small bottle of gasoline. Flames leap upward. The fire accentuates Mrs. Ralston's cheekbones and makes her face seem skeletal. A vein throbs in her neck. The young man returns to his flirtations.

People emerge like ghosts from the cane, their faces both golden and shadowed. A woman wearing a large straw hat throws more wood onto the fire. Laughter bursts like sparks in the night. The old man shouts something, and a line of women approach, holding each other at the waist, weaving. They are making a sound which is neither singing nor chanting, more like a melodic sighing. The German youths take pictures.

"Raising the demon now," Stanley whispers. Elisabetta is startled. She hasn't realized he's been standing behind her.

"Is he there?" she asks.

"Just so."

"I don't see anything."

"Look real close," Stanley hisses. "Then you'll see."

Elisabetta looks again into the flames which weave against the rows of cane, which weave against the even darker night. The faces around her seem to separate from their bodies and float somewhere between fire and sky. *The night is melting,* she thinks. And now she does see him, writhing among the flames, almost like a darker fire, the cold center of everything. She walks as close as she dares.

"Are you there?" she murmurs. But even as she thinks she can clearly see him, he enfolds himself within the flames and fades.

"Don't go. Please."

He reappears, flickering, teasing.

Please don't leave, Elisabetta entreats him. *Just tell me—*

But the flames spark and hiss, and she starts. He is vanishing again; he will not stay for her. She takes the photograph of her father and Carlotta and Catherine from her purse. *This is all I have.* She throws it into the fire. More quickly than she would have thought possible, it is consumed, and they are gone. She has given up what she has treasured. But still he turns from her, mocking.

Don't, she pleads. *Come back. Please, just tell me—*

"I deserve to know," she says.

Someone is screaming. Mrs. Ralston stands with clenched hands, her mouth twisted and ugly. "Why don't you just do it?" she shouts at her husband, who holds his hands out, as if to calm her. "Why don't you just go off with her and be done with it and stop torturing me!"

"Please, Iona," he says softly. The celebrants watch, their faces impassive. Mrs. Ralston turns and points to Elisabetta.

"It's you!" Her finger is shaking. "It's you he wants! You've led him on, but you'll suffer for it." She laughs wickedly. "Oh, you will. Evil, evil girl." Elisabetta puts her hands over her ears and turns away. One of the German youths snaps her picture. *Now I too am in someone's photograph of Barbados,* she thinks. When she looks back, Ralston is leading his wife to the taxi. She sits, rigid and staring, while he talks to her. Stanley comes over and asks something, and Ralston nods. He takes his wife's hand and holds it, and after a moment she leans her head against his shoulder. But her eyes never close.

"We're leaving, mum," Stanley says to Elisabetta.

"I can't ride with her."

Stanley looks around and clucks his tongue. "Only ride back, mum."

Elisabetta sits in front, the Ralstons in back. No one says anything, until Stanley breaks the silence.

"Did you see the demon, mum?"

"Yes," Elisabetta says.

He chuckles. He is delighted. "And did he tell you what you want to know?"

Mrs. Ralston suddenly sits upright, and Elisabetta is afraid the woman will scream again. "Did I miss it?" she asks. She turns anxiously to her husband. "Did I miss something?" He shakes his head.

"If the demon don't say, then you don't give him what you treasure enough," Stanley says. He smiles at Elisabetta. "I told you that."

"It's all I had," she replies numbly.

Stanley taps his head. "He knows."

When they arrive back at the Lime House, Mrs. Ralston formally bids them all good night, as if nothing has happened. Head held high, she goes before her husband into the hotel.

"I'm sorry," Ralston tells Elisabetta.

"Are you going to leave her?"

He looks puzzled. "I never have. Why should I now?"

Elisabetta sits in front of the vanity mirror. She wipes the traces of the fire from her face with a cleansing tissue. The alcohol stings and reminds her of childhood antiseptics. She stares at her image in the mirror, considers. The demon is gone. They are all gone—in death, in fire, in memory. There is no one left to search for or mourn.

We were all beautiful, she thinks, *and still you left us.*

Elisabetta leans closer to the mirror, and feels freedom like a cold wind. Extracting the blade from her razor, she presses its edge, thin as a feather, against her cheekbone, then draws it down, softly at first, testing. She feels nothing, and so presses deeper, until a thin red line appears, then draws the blade from cheekbone to chin in an arc finer than memory, finer than love. She watches as blood flows along the cut that will leave an even finer scar, one that could be hidden with makeup or left revealed for all to see, as she—and only she—chose.

Behind her, the curtains billow in the mirror. She smiles.

"Are you there now?" she murmurs. "Are you?"

Tidewatcher

I've been spending a lot of time at the beach lately, even though it's winter, and cold and windy, so that most days I never get out of my car. I run the heater, and watch the tide come and go according to some schedule I've never understood. Some days it's quite high and laps the shore about thirty yards from the parking area; other days, at the same hour, it's already gone out, leaving the shore denuded for as much as a hundred yards. When it comes in, it deposits the carcasses of the dead and vanished—fish, gulls, an occasional seal, not to mention the shells and carapaces of other creatures; when it goes out, it leaves a shore studded with broken glass, empty milk bottles, a container of mascara, a child's cast-off shoe. Gulls and terns search for food out there where the ocean meets the sand, and I—a middle-aged man in cap and gloves—watch them through a windshield that is always misting.

I'm coming to the shore because lately I've been uneasy about something, and I don't know what it is. Sometimes that uneasiness almost becomes a fear—of what, I again don't know. I can't explain this well. It's as if something in my life that was so firmly anchored that I took its presence for granted has slipped away and receded from me, just as surely as the tide. And just as I can never say exactly when the tide shifts, on which wave it begins moving out as opposed to moving in, so I can't say exactly when this shift in my life, this flowing away, began. One day I awoke, and it had gone, and I felt like a boy standing on a beach, alone and afraid.

Now—it's not death I'm afraid of. I've considered that— it would be natural, I suppose—but I'm really not terribly afraid of dying. Death, after all, is a natural process: it happens to everyone and everything, and always will. How can one be afraid of a natural process? It's like fearing the moon rising, or the wind in the trees, or the droning of crickets. We make the mistake of taking death personally, individually, whereas it's really quite impersonal. I, for one, find that impersonality almost comforting.

No, it's something else I'm uneasy about.

Coming to the beach calms me. The monotony of the waves is comforting, yes. But I also feel it's important for me to be here, to watch and wait, as if something might be revealed to me only here, and among the waves I could see what it is I fear and could find what it is I've lost.

I'm not alone in my vigil. Others come here, too. There are the teenagers on school lunch break who sit scrunched together, six or more to a car, if the weather is cold. If it's warmer, they stand outside, chattering and preening. Occasionally one grabs another from behind in a sort of backwards

embrace. And there are the two young women who eat sandwiches and smoke and play their car radio loudly. And the
two gay men who walk their Dobermans and survey the rest
of us with glances sharp as razors. There is the young man
who comes to fly kites of various shapes and sizes, and an
elderly couple who watch shore birds: she's confined to a
wheelchair which her husband, who looks like the old Duke
of Windsor, dutifully pushes. They often stop—one having
pointed out something to the other—and together they look
through their binoculars. I imagine they are in love.

And there are the lovers—a man with a mustache and sad
eyes who arrives in a red Camaro, and his lady friend, who
comes in a VW badly in need of a muffler. They are adulterers:
I know this because I've seen the unmatched rings on their
fingers. Also, they embrace too fervently, as if each were afraid
the other would vanish. They never eat lunch. They feast
upon each other, and that third thing, their affair.

But I'm the only one among them all who watches the tide,
and waits for something to happen.

And yesterday something did. The elderly bird watchers
started arguing, or rather, the wife started berating her husband, who stood in front of her, his arms crossed. Over the
wind, I couldn't hear what she was yelling. Then she began
hitting him, her upper body twisting in wide, painful arcs.
She struck his waist, his ribs, his elbows, and as she did, she
made a short gasping sound—*hunnh, hunnh*—like a boxer
expelling air. Her husband endured the blows until suddenly
he grasped the handles of the wheelchair and pushed it off
the walkway and through the sand, down toward the shore.
His tongue stuck out with exertion. His wife twisted and bit
his hand, so that blood came, yet he wouldn't relinquish his

grip. He grunted and pushed, his neck muscles tense as the sand got deeper, and finally he had to stop, exhausted. The wheelchair was canted in the sand. He turned and trudged back to the parking area, while his wife screamed, "Come back here, come back!" She shifted in the chair, and it leaned even more precariously. The husband stood on the walkway, took off his binoculars, and watched her struggle. The mustachioed man in the Camaro pointed, and his lover laughed, as did the teenagers. The gay men, back from their walk, leaned their heads together, whispered, and looked suspiciously at the woman in the wheelchair.

I got out of my car—to do what, I wasn't sure. The man with the kite walked over to the husband. "Aren't you going to go get her?" I heard him ask.

The husband nodded. "When she calms down," he said. He continued to stare at his wife through the binoculars.

The man with the kite looked disgusted. He walked over to me and held out the kite's string. "Can you hold this for just a minute?" he asked. I took the string. I thought he was going to the woman's aid, but instead he walked past me across the parking area to the rest rooms beyond. I stood holding the string of the kite, which was fish-shaped today. It pitched and yawed in the wind. And there we all were: the old woman, the old man, the lovers in the Camaro, the teenagers, and I—a middle-aged man holding a kite. Later, I thought I could have let it go and gone to help her myself. But I didn't. I held it dutifully and handed it back to the young man when he returned. By that time the husband had relented and was trudging back to his wife. Straining as before, he pushed her back to the parking area. She put her arms around his neck as he lifted her gently into the front

seat of their van. They left, and then the lovers left, each in
their separate car, and then the teenagers, and finally the man
with the kite. No one was left but me, who sat in my car,
thinking. I felt there was something here I should understand,
but I couldn't figure it out. It gnawed on me, and made me
uneasy. I waited for it to reveal itself, but it refused to, escaping like water through a sand channel. I turned my atten-
tions once more seaward. Waiting for the tide to change, I
let it pass.

The Man with Picasso's Eyes

*T*he girl in front of him at the water cooler had said it. She'd been bending over, drinking, one hand carefully holding back the long blond hair that smelled of shells, sun on wood, walnuts. Her friend, a pudgy girl who squinted as if trying to read some far-away sign, waited for her. Both were dressed in the loose-fitting long skirts which, Charles noted, had replaced last year's tailored look among the young women of the Trade Center.

The smell of her hair intoxicated him, evoking images of summer afternoons when one could come and go as one pleased, and there was no name for time. Charles must have been standing too close; when the girl turned, she bumped into him.

"Oh, I'm sorry," she said, her hand touching his coat, withdrawing. Water glistened on the down of her upper lip.

And then she said, "You know, you've got eyes like Picasso." Her voice lifted at the end so that later he wasn't sure whether she'd been questioning it even as she spoke.

Astonished, Charles mumbled, "I do?" And before he could ask *Why? Why do you say that?* the young woman and her companion were walking toward the banks of escalators that disgorged the Center's workers into the city streets. Charles watched them vanish into the crowd with his now painterly eyes. He stared at his reflection in the chrome surface of the water cooler, but its concavity distorted his face and made his eyes seem far away. On his way home, he kept glancing at them in the rearview mirror.

There's something here I haven't seen before, Charles thought.

When he pulled into his driveway, he saw that the automatic sprinklers were once again soaking the evening paper. He'd told the newsboy to leave it in the driveway. But they kept changing newsboys on him: he would call the last one only to be told by a pleading preadolescent voice that he was no longer his carrier. Charles gathered that his route was not very popular, either too long, or too circuitous, or too unrewarding—reasons that resulted in his paper being periodically soaked. This evening he decided to let it soak.

Let it turn to mulch, he thought.

He smelled charcoal and chemicals upon entering the house. "Carol?" he called. The only response was the barking of the puppy they'd bought last week to replace their terrier, run over by an acned teenager who, to his credit, had stopped and stood dumbly with Charles as they watched its dying tremors. His son, Josh, had cried, so they'd gotten this new puppy, still unnamed and—judging from the white powdered area on the rug—still unhousebroken. Strangely, the barking seemed to be coming from the closet. He opened it. The puppy rolled over and whined in delight. Charles closed the door; the puppy renewed its yowling.

Why is the dog in the closet? he wondered. At that moment, Josh ran down the stairs and out the door, saying as he passed, "The dog's done it again and Mom's locked him up, so don't let him out."

"Why won't he do it in there?" Charles asked, but Josh, like the girl at the water cooler, was already gone.

He found Carol in the kitchen, her head stuck in the oven. Rump thrust out, half-swallowed in its maw, she was scraping burnt grease with an X-Acto knife. Scrape, scrape.

This is she, the woman I married, Charles thought. He watched, silent as an owl, trying to remember her face before she vanished forever into the oven. He thought of fairy tales: Hansel and Gretel pushing the witch into the oven; the young girl escaping the Baba Yaga's cooking pot. Charles wanted to call her by another name, not Carol. He would call her Agnes; he would call her Lorelei; he would call her by any of a thousand names which weren't hers. If he only knew it, he would call her by the name of the girl at the water cooler who had skipped away with her friend.

"Hi," she said, not turning. "The dog's in the doghouse again."

"He's in the closet, actually," Charles said. "I'm glad you didn't leave it for me to clean up like yesterday."

"Thought you'd appreciate that." She chopped at the caked grease. "I've been working on this damn thing all afternoon. It didn't light again. I tried to fix it myself, and then I saw how dirty it was. So I decided to clean it." She held up a sooty hand for him to see. "But it still won't light. You're going to have to call the oven guy again."

Charles winced, the repairman's vinegary face before him. Twice he'd been called back; each time the return was more grudging. Charles hated dealing with mechanics, plumbers, repairmen of all kinds. He'd never mastered the proper good-fellow—yet no-nonsense—tone to use with them.

Carol returned to the oven. "So how was the day?"

"Okay." Charles poured a glass of tomato juice from the thankfully still humming refrigerator. "I've been told I have Picasso's eyes."

"Picasso, like the painter?"

"Yep."

Carol emerged from the oven, a bit of charcoal stuck to her cheek like a fly. She looked at him.

"There's no percentage in that," she said. "There's no percentage in that at all."

Charles drank his tomato juice, imagining it blood. "I don't know what she meant," he said. "Maybe it means I'm sexy."

"Of course you're sexy. Look at me"—she spread her arms, her shirt sweat-stained at the neck and armpits—"I'm sexy too. We're both enormously sexy people. But I don't know about you and Picasso. The eyes, I mean." She studied him. "Maybe Milton Berle. Who's she?"

"She?"

"She who told you about your eyes."

Charles was pleased Carol was taking an interest. Before replying, he washed his glass in the sink. "Somebody I bumped into at the water cooler. Actually, she bumped into me. It all happened so quickly, I couldn't even ask her what she meant."

"What's to ask? She thinks your eyes are like Picasso's."

"I don't even know what his eyes look like."

"Hot as coals," Carol said, pointing her knife at him. "Hot, sexy eyes. But short. Very short." She cackled and reentered the oven.

They are insatiable, Charles thought. *The things of my life want to devour me.* He looked out the kitchen window to the azalea bushes that needed trimming. He squinted, compressing both the bushes and the blue-paneled walls of his neighbor's house into planes of color, imagining them as Picasso might. A bush would no longer be a bush, but a pink-and-green salamander of color, tender, roseate. It was all in the way one saw things.

"Can you take Josh to the library tonight?" Carol asked, her voice hollow within the oven. "He's got overdue books."

"Why doesn't he just ride over on his bike?"

"No—this is the Fremont Street branch he's got to go to."

"Why does he have books from the Fremont Street branch? That's way over on the Southside."

"We couldn't find one he wanted here. They had it there, so I took him over. Then he got the others."

"Don't they have interlibrary loans for that kind of thing? I mean, why did you have to go yourself? That's a bad area of town. I don't like you going over there."

"Oh, it's perfectly safe in daytime," Carol said. She applied more Easy-Off to the oven's side.

"Well, I'm scared to go there. Day or night."

"Okay, I'll go, then."

Caught, Charles thought. He sighed. "I'll take him over after dinner."

"He's into bugs now."

"Bugs, great." He stopped at the kitchen door. "Why couldn't they just send the books to our branch?"

"He wanted them that day, I think."

"Nobody can wait for anything anymore," Charles said.

They ate a cold supper. After Charles had done the dishes, he and Josh got into Carol's van to drive to the library. Charles enjoyed driving the van. Perched high above the traffic, he could peer into the cars below. His view from above seemed royal, privileged. *I might have been happy as a truck driver,* he thought. Often he waved to them as they, higher still, passed by; sometimes they waved back. He imagined driving through America at night, CB crackling in the humid air, coffee and powdered doughnuts, weigh stations and highway patrolmen. *Smokies,* he corrected himself. Or were they still called that? He tried to recall trucking songs, but the only one that came to mind was "Six Days on the Road." Trucking didn't seem to spawn songs like those of the cowboy and lumberjack and sailor. Maybe the job was too solitary. There was no one to sing to, and thus no need for song.

They entered the Southside. Men stood in small groups outside bars and convenience stores, laughing and shouting at one another. Some leaned over the windows of parked cars and talked softly to whoever was within. A man in a shiny purple shirt danced a small jig, humming to himself. Somewhere a bottle broke. Charles looked to see whether Josh's door was locked.

"Pawn shop," Josh said.

"Pawn shop?"

"Over there." Josh pointed to a shop they'd just passed, its neon sign blinking erratically in anticipation of evening.

Charles had been noticing that lately Josh had begun to name the obvious. "There's a water tower," he'd say, as they passed one. That which had a sign was read; that which didn't was named. His son, who at age eight had seemed so innocently wise, so full of sympathetic intelligences and bemusements, had at age nine become a simpleton.

"FORTUNES TOLD," Josh read. The sign was painted on a peeling door frame. "LOVE AND WORK. YOU CAN GET AHEAD."

Love and Work, Charles marveled. He wondered whether a graduate student in psychology, frustrated by the search for an academic job, had decided that fortune-telling was an allied—possibly more remunerative—field, and so had set up shop here, complete with robe and fright wig.

"CHECKS CASHED," Josh read on a grocery store. "Don't you have to do that at a bank, Charles?"

Charles considered. "Yes. Usually you do do that at a bank. But a lot of poor people don't have bank accounts, so they have to do it in places like that." He paused. "And why, may I ask, are you calling me 'Charles,' Josh?"

"It's your name," Josh mumbled. "BAIL BONDS, TWENTY-FOUR HOURS," he read.

Charles sighed. "No, it's not. It's 'Dad.' Have you forgotten?"

Josh shifted in his seat. "Ricky Crone calls his dad 'Bill.'"

Ricky Crone, Charles thought. A mousy boy who always looked as if he'd been pulling wings off grasshoppers. His father was a medical products salesman. Every morning he put two black sample cases in the trunk of his Volvo, and every evening he removed them.

"One time I had them on the front seat, and they broke

into the damn car," he'd told Charles. "Right through the window. Drug-crazed kids. Maniacs."

"Ricky Crone can call his dad 'Pocahontas,' for all I care," Charles told Josh. "But you call me 'Dad.' No 'Charles.'"

"Mom calls you 'Charles,' and we're one big happy family," Josh countered.

"We're a *small* happy family. Do you call Mom 'Carol'?"

Josh shuffled the books in his lap. Charles noted one of the titles: *A Boy's Book of Beetles*. He shuddered. Soon insect jars would appear, and the house—so lately redolent of charcoal and dog doo—would smell like carbon tetrachloride, or worse. Josh would now possess the Power of Death—Charles saw it emblazoned in capital letters in circus wagon script. Josh would never again be innocent; the murder of beetles would corrupt him. He might even gas Carol and him as they slept. Charles imagined the two of them pinned against the felt backing of a specimen case. *This is Charles and Carol,* Josh is saying to the amazed onlookers. *My parents.*

"Does Ricky Crone call his mother"—Charles tried to remember her name, but couldn't—"whatever her name is?"

"Don't know," Josh mumbled.

"Well, why don't we just go back to what we've always done in your short little life, okay? You call me 'Dad,' and I'll call you 'Josh.' Carol is 'Mom'—I mean, Mom is 'Mom.' We'll just let it go at that, okay?"

"Okay," Josh said amicably.

Heat waves from the pavement followed them into the Fremont Street Library. The air-conditioning was broken, and all the windows were open. The sounds of the street—horns, dribbled basketballs, shouts and whistles—drifted inside. A large fan on the circulation desk stirred the heat into small liquid puddles. The library was almost empty. A librarian sat at the desk, craning her neck like a goose to receive the fan's breeze when it rotated toward her. Another filed away books from a cart. Two small black children knelt on chairs and fought to see who would turn the pages of the book they were reading. A middle-aged lady with wispy hair, legs crossed primly at the ankles, held her book stiffly before her, as if she found either its smell or its contents repellent.

Charles went to the Fine Arts section and looked for Picasso. He found one book of Picasso's drawings and another on the painter's Blue Period. Both had photographs of the authors on the dust jackets, but neither had a picture of Picasso. Charles looked at the check-out dates in the books: no one, it seemed, was very interested in the painter.

His question seemed to annoy the librarian at the front desk.

"Picasso's life wouldn't be in the *Art* section," she said. "Lives are in Biography." She pointed. "Over there. The 92's." She returned to her communion with the fan.

Charles found two books on Picasso. The first was a thin volume with thick type. Once again, the paintings were featured, although there were a few shots of Picasso wedged between revelers in a cafe, standing in a crowd at a bullring, almost hidden behind some tall canvases in his studio. In none of them could Charles clearly see his eyes.

This book should really be in the Arts section, but I won't tell her, Charles thought mischievously.

The second book was better. A large section of photographs showed Picasso sitting at dinner with friends, imitating a bull for the camera, walking along a bridge in Paris, standing in the middle of an exhibition. In the last one, he seemed shy, as if surprised by the camera and bewildered at what to do. And there were more: Picasso painting with light, the sketch created in the very air through time-lapse photography; Picasso at the kitchen table feeding a cat from his plate; Picasso in a French sailor's shirt sitting under a tree in Arles. In this photograph he stared straight ahead, intense yet remote, as if the act of staring were a pose, a mask. The eyes were wide, almost empty, yet smoldered from some darkness within. They seemed mocking. Charles turned the page.

In the next photograph Picasso was walking with his mistress on a beach in southern France. He held a parasol over her head to protect her from the sun, as if she were a queen arrived on a caravan and he an adoring retainer. She was a good bit taller than Picasso, Charles noted, which is why he held the parasol so high, increasing the illusion of homage. The woman's beach dress gently hugged her thigh. A warm perfume seemed to float through the photograph. Picasso was smiling. And as Charles looked at the picture, the evening's limpid heat, the squeals of brakes and children, the smell of hamburgers and tired asphalt that drifted through the windows—all seemed to diminish and fade away.

Love, Charles thought. *The world can be loved*. Everything was only possibility, in anticipation of love: the world seen through his—and Picasso's—eyes. He would take the book home; he would show Carol.

He smiled at the sullen librarian as he and Josh checked out their books. He looked at his son's choices: *Constructing Small Animal Traps, Jungle Beasts I Have Known, Snakes of North America*. From insects, he'd moved to bigger prey.

Charles decided to take the expressway back even though

the trip would be longer. He felt electric, unfettered, and wanted to feel the illusion of flying above the city streets that the expressway offered. The van merged with the great river of traffic. Josh browsed through his books and Charles let his mind bob like a cork. He was in Paris, in Arles, on the beach in southern France. He was everywhere he'd never been, and yet he was also here, where the neon lights and signs along the road were winking at him and the passing cars cheered him on.

"Dad, could you see a rattlesnake before it struck?" Josh asked.

"I don't see how that matters," Charles replied. "There aren't any rattlesnakes around here."

Josh held up the book. "This says they're all over America."

"They're mostly in wilder places, Josh. The woods. Snakes don't like to be around people."

"If I was in the woods—could I see one before it struck?"

"That's why they've got rattles," Charles said. "To warn you off."

"Well—if I came on one real suddenly, would he get a chance to rattle first?"

"I don't know, Josh. Why worry about it? You're not going to the woods anytime soon."

"Have you ever seen a rattler?"

"In a zoo, I guess." Charles thought. "Somewhere. A museum, maybe." It *had* been a museum—an exhibit in a glass box. He'd pushed a button, and the rattler reared its long-dead head and for five seconds shook its rattle.

"Hey, Dad, that woman's naked!"

Charles started, the rattlesnake collapsing into an inert coil. "What?" he said.

Josh pointed to a yellow Honda that had just passed them on the passenger side and was now zipping through traffic like a merry badger. In the deepening twilight Charles saw the outline of a woman's head, the last light scattering on her long blond hair.

"That woman in the yellow car was naked," Josh repeated.

"What are you talking about, Josh? People don't drive around naked."

"Well, she was. I saw."

"How could you see?"

"She slowed down beside us until the other car went ahead. I could look in. I saw."

"What? What did you see?"

"I told you. She was naked."

"Josh, that's crazy. She must've just looked naked. She must've had something on." Charles searched for possibilities: a small bikini, a flesh-colored body stocking. Unconsciously he accelerated, trying to keep the darting little car in sight.

"Nope." Josh shook his head. "Naked."

"She had to have *something* on."

"Just her hair," Josh said. He returned to his snake book. *How could his son be so dispassionate?* Charles wondered. He suddenly felt he was driving nowhere, his destination forgotten. Was he following her? Was he going home? Charles tried to keep the yellow Honda in sight, but it disappeared, becoming one of the many red taillights shimmering in the dusk.

Almost pruriently, he wanted to ask Josh *exactly* what he saw, but he didn't. Instead, he said, "Why do you suppose she was naked, Josh?" *He should be asking me this,* Charles thought, and was shamed. As Carol would say, there was no percentage in this.

"Maybe she was hot. Hey, Dad, could you turn the light on so I can keep reading?"

Charles flicked it on and glanced at his son. Josh was focusing his attention upon the venomous water moccasin, confined—thankfully—to the southern regions of North America.

"Let's see that one," Charles said. Josh held up the book. Charles committed the coloration and patterns to memory. If he ever came across a water moccasin, he would be ready.

A few last rags of color hung in the sky when they arrived home. Charles carefully parked the van between Josh's bike and that of some other child—probably Ricky Crone with his first-name father. He was still thinking about the naked lady, imagining himself also naked in the car beside her, both of them riding into the moon. But she was gone, and anyway, he hadn't really seen her. He left the Picasso book in the van and followed Josh inside.

The kitchen was dark. The smell of Easy-Off reminded him first of hospital corridors, then of sexual unguents and jellies. He opened the oven. The light came on happily to reveal clean ribbed surfaces. He thought of Carol's rump sticking out as she'd cleaned the oven. Didn't people who committed suicide by putting their heads in stoves realize how absurd they'd look when found? Why didn't that stop them?

He looked out the kitchen window, but there was no longer anything to see—flowers, bushes, his neighbor's blue wall, everything that had color had merged into shades of black and gray. On his way into the living room he opened the closet door; the puppy was gone. He found Carol curled in a chair, drinking a lemon tonic, cutting her toenails. *This is she,* Charles thought. *The woman I married. My only wife.*

She looked up. "So you made it back okay? No gangs stomp you?"

"Nope," Charles said affably. He sat in the leather chair opposite her and pulled the lamp chain. "I did see a naked lady, though." He didn't know why he said this, because of course he hadn't seen her.

"Now that's pretty interesting. Just where did you see her?"

"On the expressway. She was driving a car. Stark naked. Can you believe it?"

"Really?" Carol was looking at him, Charles thought, with respect.

"Maybe she wasn't really naked. She passed by so quickly. Probably wearing some flesh-colored bikini." He was embarrassed now that he'd brought it up: the vision, after all, had never been his.

"You've had some interesting experiences with women today, lover," Carol said.

"Oh—" Charles waved his hand. "I don't know." He hesitated. "I looked at some books on Picasso at the library. I've decided my eyes don't look anything like his."

"You should've checked one out," Carol said. "I would've liked to have seen too. Maybe we've been missing something."

After Carol went to bed, Charles stepped into the backyard. From inside the garage, he heard the puppy whine. "Hush," he said. He looked at the stars, or—more exactly—he looked where he knew them to be, obscured as they were by the greenish glow of the city. As a child he'd lived in a small town farther north. What was not town was field, and what was

not field was woods, thick and beckoning. He'd often ex-
plored the woods, but had slept outdoors only once, in a field
with two other boys. When they turned off their flashlights,
there had been thousands of stars, and that seemed only proper,
his due. Something had diminished since then, he decided.
Some things could no longer be seen at all.

Charles decided he would take Josh to the country soon.
They would go for a hike. Josh would worry about snakes,
but of course would never find any, nor would any find him.
They might even sleep out. He would introduce Josh to the
stars, if they were still there. He would show his son something. It was the best he could do.

"Oh, I *should* have seen her," he said aloud to no one.

When he went into the bedroom, Carol was asleep, one
leg stretched across his side. He watched for a moment to
make sure she was breathing: she breathed very lightly when
asleep, and sometimes he was fearful that she'd stopped entirely. Satisfied she was still alive, he brushed his teeth and
came to bed. When he closed his eyes, he once again saw the
face of the girl at the water cooler, but she was no longer at
the water cooler; she was walking naked along a beach, while
he—her foolish servant—held an umbrella over her head.
Charles turned sleepily to his own, his real wife, and touched
her, but the umbrella was growing larger, covering her and
him as well. Then he shut his artist's eyes and let her drive
away down the expressway, while he on his beach closed his
eyes and, still holding the umbrella for her on whatever sands
she chose to walk, hunkered down and made shelter.

Anne Rey

When Anne Rey was a little girl and her mother read her fairy tales from a large purple book, her favorites had been those in which the hero embarked on a journey by boat; in later years, after consulting the I Ching, Anne always felt a special thrill when she received a hexagram advising "crossing a great sea." So perhaps it was not surprising that shortly after her mother began complaining about the "funny little hat" on the side of her head, Anne Rey—twenty-eight years old, single, an art restorer specializing in prints and drawings—decided to give up her small apartment and move onto a sailboat.

Her mother had just undergone a battery of skull X-rays, angiograms, and CT scans. "Sometimes the sensation of scalp tingling or phantom pressure comes from a brain tumor," the neurologist, a Dr. Gans, told Anne. "Maybe malignant, maybe not. I'd hoped that's what it was." He saw her expression.

"I don't mean I *hoped* we'd find something, you understand. But now I can't tell you anything." He gestured to the ghostly films of Anne's mother's skull on the light box behind him. "There's nothing there."

"What's going to happen?" Anne asked.

"What can I tell you? There's no pathology. No pathology, no prognosis." He leaned back in his chair. "Maybe it's psychosomatic. Maybe it'll go away."

Anne looked at the films of her mother's skull and felt she was staring into realms of light and shadow that she had never known existed.

Dr. Gans leaned forward, his chair creaking. "Look—if it's real, it'll show up eventually. If it's not"—he shrugged—"well, let's just wait and see."

Two days later Anne Rey began looking for a sailboat on which to live. She spent an afternoon at the marinas putting up neatly typed notices in ships' chandleries, sailing schools, convenience stores, and laundromats:

> BOAT SITTER. RESPONSIBLE PROFESSIONAL WOMAN WILL
> GUARD YOUR BOAT AND PERFORM LIGHT SERVICE IN
> EXCHANGE FOR LIVING ON IT. IMPECCABLE REFERENCES.

And she left her phone number.

She received three calls: one from a man who soon made it clear he wanted Anne to live with *him* on his boat; another from a woman who wanted rent, despite the clarity of Anne's notice. The third caller identified himself as Lou from the Ship-Shape Shop in Long Beach.

"You asked me if you could put up a notice, remember? I was putting beer in the cooler."

"Oh, sure," Anne said.

"You want to boat-sit, right? Well, I was over at San Pedro yesterday, out by the number two marina. Me and a friend got a hull-cleaning business, part-time. The guy whose hull we were doing said he had a friend who was going on a long trip and wanted his hull cleaned while he was gone. And he was worried about his boat being broken into. I told him I knew somebody who wanted to boat-sit, if his friend was interested. Well, he called him, and the friend's interested. I can give you his number, if you like."

"That's great," Anne said.

"It's a real nice boat, from what I hear. Thirty-eight foot Coronado. That's counting the bowsprit. It'd be real nice for one person. There's just you, right? That's what I told him."

"Just me," Anne said.

Adam Samuelson, the boat's owner, was an entertainment contract lawyer who wore glasses frames too big for his eyes and sandals too big for his feet, so that they flip-flopped against the pavement as he walked. He was fascinated with Anne's being an art restorer.

"Like old masters, right?"

"Well, not really," Anne said. "I just handle prints and drawings. An occasional watercolor. Oils and tempera I don't do at all."

"I didn't know you guys got so specialized," Samuelson said.

He wondered why she wanted to live on a boat.

"I've wanted to since I was a child," Anne said. "And now's

a good time. I feel like I need to simplify things, get more control. You know, make things smaller."

"It's small, all right," he laughed.

They went to see the boat, the *Estelle*. "It used to be *Esther*, after my first wife," Samuelson said. "But I had to change it when I remarried. Lucky I could still use the first three letters." The boat moved languidly in its slip, held fast by anchor and spring lines. The mast creaked slightly as it bobbed; its stays hummed in the breeze. Below, it was much lighter than Anne had expected, due to several oversized portholes. The main compartment consisted of a galley ("Good stove, always lights"), a chart table, and long side couchettes which transformed into a dining table. There was a head in the forward compartment ("No shower, but you can take them free up at the marina") and a large captain's quarters aft, with bunk beds, built-in lockers, and a small fold-down desk. Everything seemed close at hand, manageable. Anne ran her fingers along the wood paneling; as if responding to her touch, the *Estelle* rocked gently, cradling her. Anne felt safe.

"Like I told you, it's small," Samuelson said, misinterpreting her silence.

"I want it that way," Anne replied. "It's wonderful."

Within a week, Anne had moved aboard the *Estelle*. She held a yard sale which rid her of much of her furniture, appliances, and wardrobe. Goodwill collected still more. She donated most of her books to the local branch of the Los Angeles City Library and gave her records to a friend. What could neither be kept, given away, nor sold was boxed and taken to her studio basement. Anne came to the *Estelle* with two suitcases, a garment bag, half a box of books, a print of Ulrich's *Etcher in His Studio,* and a cassette player with some of her favorite records dubbed onto tape. She put the print over the chart table, her clothes in the built-in drawers and lockers. The books fit neatly into the shelf along the bunk bed. She examined the charts rolled up in pigeonholes under the table. She liked the one of Avalon Harbor West, so she unfurled it along the table and clamped it flat with the parallel rulers on one end and a spring clamp on the other. Everything was in its place. Anne was satisfied.

She called her mother from the pay phone at the marina.

"They won't tell me anything at the hospital," her mother said. "I think they know I've got something bad—but they won't tell me."

"Mom, I've spoken with Dr. Gans. They really can't find anything wrong. Be glad."

"Well, I know there's something wrong, even if they don't. But I think they do. They look at me funny. They whisper."

Anne sighed. "Mom, that's not so. You've got to quit talking that way."

Her mother was silent.

"You still feel it?" Anne asked. "The little hat?"

"Oh, you know—I put it on, I take it off."

Anne didn't like the way the conversation was going. "I've moved onto my boat," she said.

"Oh, really?"

"Yep. Just finished. It's nice. You'll have to come down and see."

"Where are you calling from? I thought you weren't going to get a phone."

"I'm not. I'm calling from a pay phone at the marina."

"I don't like you not having a phone. What if I have to get in touch with you in the evening?"

"You can call the marina. Somebody's there till eleven. And you can always leave a message on the answering machine at the studio."

"By the time you get all these messages," her mother said, "it could be too late."

"What do you mean, Mom?"

"If there was an emergency."

"What emergency?" Anne laughed nervously. "Are you planning on having an emergency?"

"You never know."

Anne rubbed her hand across her forehead. "Mom—it frightens me when you talk like this."

And now her mother laughed. "Well," she said, "I wouldn't know you cared."

Anne made herself a cup of hot chocolate after the phone call, and while the gas stove hissed, she pondered all her mother had said. Its meaning disturbed, yet eluded her. Like the X-rays on Dr. Gans' light box, either something was there—unseen—or was not there at all. "I can't think about this now," Anne said aloud: talking to herself was something she'd recently begun doing. She took her hot chocolate to the captain's quarters, read a few pages from *Swann's Way*—her summer reading project—and felt cozy and snug. She was soon lulled to sleep by the *Estelle*'s gentle rolling.

The Callot engraving sent over from the Oldershaw Galleries puzzled Anne. From the French school of the late sixteenth century, it depicted a landscape with two farmers pulling a heavy plow. Clouds roiled above the fields in thick fibrous masses. On the left side of the engraving, near the rooftops of a distant village, a reddish stain had appeared; several smaller ones dotted the fields. Anne had never seen stains like these. No mold, climactic condition, or pollution of which she was aware had caused them. She thumbed through Plenderleith's *Conservation of Antiquities and Works of Art,* but had no luck identifying them. Anne put on a Bach violin partita and looked at the Callot through a magnifying glass over the light box. She shook her head, and brushed back strands of blond hair that fell over the magnifier.

"Well, there's got to be a cause," she said aloud. "It's got to be something." She put a beaker of water for coffee on the hot plate where she heated chemical solutions. Gingerly, Anne touched the largest of the red stains; it was just the size of her fingertip. She drew back her finger and looked at it, half expecting to see the stain transferred there, then went over to the sink and washed her hands until the skin burned. "Crazy," she murmured. She sat down with her coffee. She decided to send photographs of the Callot to her old mentor, Preston Hamblin, at the Columbia Academy for Conservation in New York. Restless then, Anne paced the studio. "I don't want to work anymore today," she said. She turned on her answering machine and returned to the *Estelle.* She tried to take a nap, but kept thinking about the Callot. Still restless, Anne got up and ran the engine to recharge the boat's batteries, and after that waited for night to come.

Summer evenings on the *Estelle* became a solace for Anne Rey. More and more she left the studio early to return to the boat, picking up something along the way to cook for dinner. After a shower, she changed into jeans or cotton shorts and a workshirt and sat with a beer in Samuelson's deck chair that said HOTSHOT LAWYER on the back. As shadows spread like oil across the water, Anne watched the harbor come to life. Arc lights illuminated the great ships' holds, exposed like the gutted ribbing of monstrous sea creatures. Giant cranes lifted pallets of boxes, crates, barrels, sometimes entire railway cars. The ships were often overhauled at night, and workers in canvas slings and gleaming helmets swung like acrobats against the hulls, acetylene torches sparking wildly. The water wove a silent cocoon around everything, while the evening light flattened the scene into a mezzotint. Anne watched until the breeze became too chill. Then she went below, put on her hooded sweatshirt, and climbed into her bunk in the captain's quarters to read until she fell asleep. The *Estelle* rocked in the slip, gently groaning and creaking. Anne's childhood seemed very near in the small cabin: footsteps on a porch, a hand on the bedroom door, adult voices heard through walls and floors—all seemed redeemable just beyond the wooden hull. Here she could sleep, guarded and protected.

No one ever came to the boat, and it suited her.

Her mother refused to come. "I'm afraid of water," she told Anne over the phone.

"Mom, what are you talking about? You've never been afraid before."

"You should be too. Boats sink, you know."

"Not in a harbor, Mom. I'm tied to the dock. It's safe."

Her mother grunted skeptically.

Anne sighed. "How are you feeling, Mom?"

"My head hurts."

"It hurts?"

"Yes."

"Where the little hat was?"

"There—and other places, too."

"What does the doctor say?" Anne asked anxiously.

"Nothing."

"He doesn't say anything?"

"No—he says it's nothing. It's always nothing."

"Well, thank God," Anne said, relieved.

"But I know he's lying."

"Oh, Mom—not this again." Anne was exasperated.

"I can tell. I can see them passing signals to each other."

"Mom, that's crazy!"

"I know what I know," her mother said smugly.

"You've got to stop thinking that. Please."

Her mother was silent.

"Please, Mom. Promise me you'll stop thinking this."

"Do you remember Cleo Springs?" her mother asked.

Cleo Springs. It was where they had lived in Oklahoma before Anne's father died when she was three. After that, they'd moved to California, staying with a great-aunt until her mother found work as a bank secretary.

"I got stung under the eye by a wasp," Anne said. "That's all I remember."

"We lived in a white frame house with a big porch that ran all the way around it. I loved that porch. I'd sit with you, and we'd watch the rain come down. You'd try to grab the rain. I'd lean over the porch railing with you, and you'd reach for it. Do you remember?"

"No."

"Well—you did." Her mother sighed. "I don't know why you changed."

"What do you mean, Mom?"

"You don't care about things anymore. You don't care about me."

"Mom—that's just not true. You know that's not true."

"I know what I know."

"Don't say that!" Anne snapped.

"That's the only place I've ever really been happy," her mother said softly. "On that porch. What a shame it came at the beginning of my life."

Anne was staring again at the Callot: the stains always seemed to be getting larger. At least once a day, she would take out her triangular scale and measure them, but they never changed. The phone rang, and she jumped. It was Preston Hamblin from the Columbia Academy for Conservation. His voice was as she remembered it—austere, partrician, as dry as a leaf in autumn. Anne imagined him sitting in his Shaker chair, cigarette burning in the ashtray beside him.

"I've examined your Callot photographs," he said, "and I've made some inquiries. I think I have at least a partial answer. But it's not good, I'm afraid."

"Okay," Anne said.

"Yes, well." Hamblin cleared his throat. "You know that during the sixteenth century papers were made that often had a high acidic content. The fibers tend to disintegrate over time if not properly preserved—magnesium carbonate and all that. But there are certain kinds of paper from this period that are more troublesome. Especially a batch made around 1645 in the mills at Fontainebleau."

"Fontainebleau," Anne repeated. She wrote it down.

"We don't really know what the basis of the acid is in that paper, but it shows itself as those reddish stains. You don't usually run into it in prints of the period, although my friends at the Huntington say it's quite common in books printed then. Well, you see where I'm leading. Callot must have gotten ahold of some. Usually he used a better quality paper. The Courtauld ran into some Le Creuzes like this a few years back. Had everybody scratching their heads."

"What can I do?" Anne asked.

"I'm not sure. It's given everybody a problem, I know. But—I'll be talking to my friends at the Courtauld soon, and I'll ask how they've come along with it. And I'll get back with you."

"Thanks so much," Anne said.

"So—how is sunny California?"

"Fine. I'm living on a boat now."

"Ah—" Hamblin said. "How sybaritic."

Some days later Anne's mother called at the studio. "I just don't feel right," she said, "and I can't pretend I don't. There's something bad wrong with my head."

"What is it, Mom? Is it the headaches?"

"No. This is worse. There's something growing inside me. It's pushing my brains out." She sounded in tears. "I've tried not to think about it. I didn't want to bother you."

"I'll come over," Anne said.

When she arrived her mother was sitting calmly in her wing chair and sipping black cherry tea. She seemed smaller, more frail, and she blinked when Anne came in, as if she couldn't quite see her.

"How are you, Mom?" Anne asked.

Her mother shrugged, waved her hand. "It's all right now. I'll get used to it, I suppose. If you want some tea, you'll have to put the water on."

Anne hadn't been to her mother's apartment for three weeks. Everywhere—on the counters, the table, the floor—were Dixie cups turned upside down. She filled the kettle with water, put it on the stove, and lifted one of the cups: a cockroach slithered away, its antennae feverishly poking the air. She turned over another cup on the counter, then one on the floor. Under each, a cockroach.

She walked back into the living room. "Mom, what's this all about?" She held out one of the cups.

Her mother folded her hands primly in her lap. "I'll be honest with you. I just don't want to kill them anymore."

"You don't want to kill them?" Anne sat down.

"Oh, I guess I'd like to. But I just don't want to bother with it anymore. I've been killing cockroaches all my life."

Anne tensed, unsure what was happening. "Mom, you've got to do something with them. You can't keep putting cups over them."

She looked at Anne, a hint of challenge in her eyes. "Well, what would you suggest?"

"Jesus!" Anne cried, and stood up, accidentally knocking over a cup near the sofa: the cockroach underneath didn't run, but rather stood on its hind legs, antennae twitching, as if performing a trick. Both women stared at it. It scurried away.

Anne drew a deep breath. "Mom, I think you should go back to the hospital for another checkup. If it hurts—"

"They'll say there's nothing wrong," her mother interrupted. "It's in there"—she tapped her head—"but they'll never admit it. I know that now."

"That's crazy, Mom. They haven't found anything *wrong*. Why in the name of God don't you believe them?"

"And I know why they won't admit it."

"All right—why?"

"They won't tell me because they *put* it in there." She tapped her head again. "They put it in the very first time I was in the hospital. When they gave me that test. When they gave me that injection—"

"The CT scan," Anne said numbly.

"—that's when they put it in. That's how they did it. With that needle."

"What, Mom? Put what in?"

Her mother shrugged. "What's inside me. What's making me crazy."

Staring at her mother, Anne saw the future as a large light-filled room whose great door was slowly being closed. She and her mother sat in opposite chairs outside that room, revealed to one another only by its reflected and fast-diminishing light.

"Oh, Mom—" Anne went over and knelt beside her, placing her hands on her mother's arm. The older woman's skin was dry, papery.

"Let's go back to Cleo Springs," her mother said, staring hard into Anne's eyes.

"Mom—"

She grasped Anne's arm with both hands. "I can show you where we lived. When you were a baby. I can show you everything you've forgotten." Anne shook her head. Her mother gripped her arm tightly, almost painfully. "I'll get better there."

"Mom, Mom," Anne murmured.

"Don't you want me to get better?"

Anne stood, and her mother rose with her, still holding her arm with both hands. *I will have to pry her fingers away*, Anne thought desperately. But then her mother let go, all at once, and sat back in the chair. She smiled, a smirk almost, and Anne had to look away. Pressure marks from her mother's fingers mottled her arm. Anne rubbed them, rubbed them, but they wouldn't go away.

"You only think of yourself," her mother said. "Oh, I know you now."

Anne returned to the studio and called Dr. Gans. He was in a residents' conference. "Is it an emergency?" the switchboard asked, and she said "Yes," and then quickly, "No," and left her number. *Be calm*, Anne told herself. *There are things that can be done*. She put a Handel organ concerto on the record player, made some coffee, and tried to go back to work. But she couldn't concentrate. She unscrewed jars of chemicals and forgot what formula she was preparing. Once she feared she'd put an eighteenth-century English hunting print that she was retouching into a bath for removing fox-rot, a fungus. She gave up and tried to pay bills—only to find herself staring blankly at her checkbook, unable to remember whom she was paying. Then she remembered she hadn't yet checked her answering machine. She got up and flipped it on.

There were two hang-ups, an inquiry from a client, and

then the voice of Preston Hamblin. "Yes, well...ordinarily I'd call again, but I'm off to Belgium in a bit, and I wanted to get back to you." He cleared his throat. "I've talked to my Courtauld friends, and the news, I'm afraid, is not good, not good at all. The bottom line is this: there's not much you can do with this paper. The stains can't be eradicated, and they can't be stopped. Only stabilized for a while."

"Stabilized," Anne repeated. Mechanically, she wrote it down.

Hamblin went on to outline recommendations for further treatment, which Anne tried to copy. He seemed to be speaking a language she no longer understood. While he droned on, Anne stared at the Callot on the easel. The late afternoon sunlight raked it at such an angle that the reddish stains were almost obscured; if she squinted a bit, they seemed to disappear altogether.

"...so I'd give it another two hundred years or so," Hamblin was saying. "Then it'll just be a horror. But—look on the bright side. By then maybe our techniques will be better. Science marches on, you know. I don't think the damage will ever be restorable, however. The paper has just eaten itself up, after all."

Anne turned the machine off. She looked again at the Callot.

"Just rotting away," she said. "Everything rotting, rotting, rotting."

Her mat knife lay on the workbench. Anne picked it up and approached the Callot. *I could slash it,* she thought, and just the thinking of it gave her a kind of joy. She needn't stop there, she realized. She could slash all the prints and drawings.

It would be easy. She would become an ally of time and destruction; she would become her own instrument of inevitability.

Her hands began to tremble, as if they had a quick will of their own, and Anne clenched them. She felt she might choke, and then—incredibly—she was choking and gasping for breath. Panicked, she stumbled to the sofa and lay down. Her breath came in short, harsh rasps. She tried to breathe deeply, willing calmness to return, and after some minutes, it did. She looked at her hand: the mat knife had slipped out and was lying on the floor. The Callot rested undisturbed on its easel.

"There's just nothing I can do for you," Anne said. "I'm sorry." She picked up the knife and put it on the workbench.

"I'm going to be alone soon," she murmured.

Anne returned to the *Estelle* and got under the comforter in the captain's quarters. Outside the porthole a dirty gray gull preened on a piling. Anne couldn't bear to look at it and pulled the curtain.

There is nothing to do, she thought. She could only wait for everything to happen that would happen. Anne remembered Dr. Gans's advice: *If it's real, it'll show up—let's just wait and see.* She would wait. She would see.

Anne rocked gently, the comforter wrapped around her shoulders, for what seemed like a long time. Then, cautiously, she opened the porthole curtain. The gray gull was still there, head under its wing, asleep.

She would wait. She would see. She could extend herself no further.

A Mexican Tale

*I*f anything could be said to haunt me, it is the smell of
lemons and the wind. When it blows at night across the
Canadian tundra and rattles the tin shell of the research station, I can still awaken in a hot sweat, as if I were back on
the plains of Mexico's Bolsón de Mapimí, sixteen years ago.
And then I smell the lemons, although I know I must imagine
it. I have to press my fingers hard against the cold glass of
the window by my cot to convince myself that I'm here near
the Arctic Circle, thousands of miles from the Bolsón and
from her, La Mascarilla, the witch who pursues me.

I am a cultural anthropologist, a specialist on the Ynglit
Indians of the Canadian Arctic. I hate cold climates; if you
had told me sixteen years ago that I would be spending much
of my time in one, I would've laughed. I was in the Bolsón
then, researching the Tarahumara Indians who, along with
the Yaqui, live there. I was studying the designs on their

pottery and other artifacts. I imagined I saw similarities between these and ancient Mayan designs, thus suggesting that the Tarahumara might have descended from the Maya and not from the Inca as had been supposed. I was young and had visions of revising Mexican anthropology before I was thirty.

I stayed in a small room above the post office/barbershop in Fuera, some miles west of Cuatrocienegas. In colloquial Spanish, Fuera means "Get away," which amused me. There were few other towns or villages in the Bolsón. It is a land of arid plains and bald mountains; the wind is its animating spirit. Hot and dry, it is not especially strong, but it is insistent. It insinuates itself, drying your soul into a husk, shriveling it from the inside out.

The Indians were tolerant of me. I spoke Spanish, although they usually spoke their own dialect among themselves when I was around. They were suspicious of strangers. Few came, and those who did left quickly. There was simply no reason to be in the Bolsón if you didn't already live there. My only friend was Nicanor, the barber, postmaster, and my landlord. He loved American big band music and had an extensive collection ordered from a shop in Chicago. God knows where he got the money. It was strange to sit in his small room behind the barbershop late at night and listen to Bob Norvo singing "Sentimental Journey" while staring out the window onto the ash-gray plains. Once I imagined a line of miniature camels on the horizon while Ella Fitzgerald sang "Begin the Beguine." Nicanor was amused by my researches; I must be a great scholar, he told me, to see value in these old pots. Most of life amused him, really—and he held most of it in contempt.

Two months after my arrival in Fuera, I was collecting my mail when a squad of state militia from Monterrey roared into the plaza in four jeeps. I was struck by how clean their uniforms seemed; I had already become unaccustomed to clothes that weren't stained or dyed by the reddish-gray dust of the Bolsón. The captain of the militia—a stocky man with a badly trimmed mustache and a face like an inverted pear—talked with Leopoldo Cortez, the local *guardia*, or constable. Leopoldo turned his lip out like a child who is being scolded; the captain picked at his mustache, jabbed his finger in the direction of the mountains, and swept his arms to include the plains. His troops sat in their jeeps and looked blankly about them, as if they had just awakened and were trying to figure out where they were. Some closed their eyes. Probably wishing Fuera away, I thought: either the Bolsón made a ghost of you, or you made one of it. Leopoldo and the captain got in one jeep. Gunning their engines, the squad circled the plaza and drove out of town.

I asked Nicanor what was happening. He grunted. "A bad business. There is a man, Antonio Perra, whose family has always farmed land near the Tonga Mountain. Early this year they lost this land to a big mineral company in Mexico City. They couldn't prove they legally owned it. They fought the case in Monterrey Court—even hired a lawyer, which must have been difficult for them. But they lost and were forced to quit the land. Antonio made several trips to Monterrey while the case was being judged. He made his last trip Friday, it seems. He went to the office of the lawyer who represented the mineral company and shot him in the face. Then he cut out his heart with his *cuchillero*."

I winced. Nicanor grinned. "A bad, bad business, eh? But

there's more. The lawyer's secretary had the misfortune to run in upon hearing the shot. Antonio killed her, too." He shook his head. "Bloodlust. It makes a man crazy." He looked in the direction of the militia, already swallowed up in the vastness of the plains. "They are here to find Antonio. They believe he's come back to hide among his people. They don't trust Leopoldo handling the case. As well they shouldn't."

"Will they find him?" I asked.

"Maybe. The Bolsón seems empty, my young friend, but it is also endless. A man can often stay where he is and never be found."

The militia made Fuera their base, billeting themselves in the storeroom of the cantina, where they sang and drank late into the night. In the morning, groggy and in bad temper, they stomped through the plaza, checked their guns by firing them once or twice in the air, gunned their jeeps for some minutes, then drove out of town. The captain always seemed to be haranguing Leopoldo, who sat beside him, patient and silent. Nicanor said that the captain told Leopoldo that he wished it were forty years ago. Then he could have taken a few Indians and whipped them—even shot one or two—until someone told him where Antonio was hiding.

The second Sunday after they came, I was in my room writing letters when I heard shouting in the street. To hear any loud noise in Fuera was unusual, so I went to the window, and then outside. People were gathering in clusters around the plaza. My first thought, foolishly enough, was that a parade had come to town. Then the four jeeps of the militia appeared. They moved slowly, almost cautiously, and circled the plaza with great ceremony. In the back of the second jeep, his arms locked behind him, knelt a prisoner. He was bleeding from the mouth, his face puffy and discolored, one eye swollen shut. The captain almost strutted as he got out of the jeep. He pulled at his crotch while talking to Leopoldo, who nodded dumbly. The soldiers were smiling for the first time; they had captured their man and now would be leaving this godforsaken land. The crowd stared at Antonio. He in turn stared over their heads to the plains beyond. Later Nicanor told me that Antonio had been ashamed to have been caught and trussed up like a wounded chicken in front of his people. He later lost his eye, I learned, and so was half-blind when he was executed some months later in the prison at Matamoros.

That evening, while Les Brown played "Blue Skies," I asked Nicanor how they found him. "Betrayed, what else?" he said, and laughed. "The story is almost funny." Antonio had been hiding with a cousin-in-law. The militia came early that morning and surrounded the house. Antonio tried to escape through a small window and got stuck. Two soldiers pulled him from behind while he kicked wildly. Others went around to the front of the window and beat him senseless while he was jammed there. They beat the cousin, too, and would have arrested him, but the captain decided they should return to Fuera quickly, before word of Antonio's capture spread.

"Who betrayed him?" I asked.

Nicanor shrugged and flipped over the record.

Silence settled like Bolsón dust over the whole affair. I thought little more of it and went about my collecting and cataloging. Weeks passed. I finished my preliminary research and left Fuera for three months to collate my findings and make preliminary reports to my research committee. When I returned, Nicanor greeted me as if I had just come back from an evening at the cantina. "Well, it's you," he grunted. "Back to look at more pots, I suppose. Lucky for you I've kept your room, in spite of all the people who've been demanding it." I gave him a Jack Teagarden album as a present. He snorted and helped carry my gear upstairs.

Later that evening, while Nicanor smoked and I drank a tepid beer, he filled me in on what little had happened in my absence. It was then that I learned Antonio had been executed.

"Did they ever find out who betrayed him?"

Nicanor's eyes brightened in a way I had never before seen. "Ah, there's a strange story about that. It's only a rumor, I tell you. But you will be interested. It's a story a man of learning would appreciate." He leaned closer to me in his straw chair, one hand on his knee, the other gesturing with his cigarette.

"They say that Antonio's family, desperate to find the betrayer, appealed to a local *bruja*—a witch—for help. This *bruja* is known as La Mascarilla. What her real name is no one knows. She lives some miles outside of town where the dry riverbed meets Las Gorgas Canyon. After some days she named Héctor Milla—another cousin of Antonio's—as the betrayer. How she learned this no one knows. Some say she turned herself into a crow and perched outside many windows, watching and listening." Nicanor saw the expression on my face and waved his hand. "This, of course, I don't believe.

"Milla was brought before a village council and interrogated. At first he maintained his innocence, but then the *bruja* spoke something in his ear. He became still as stone, and then began confessing his guilt. He could not lie before the witch." Nicanor sat back in his chair, folded his arms, and smiled.

"And what happened?"

Nicanor spread his hands. "Who knows? Some say he was killed, some say no. Some say the witch herself determined his fate. But"—he raised his finger dramatically—"he has never been seen again. Of course, no one admits having been personally present at this trial. Leopoldo made some inquiries, then gave up. Héctor's family is silent.

"You are a man of learning, of reason. You're not ignorant like these people"—he swept his arms wide to include the entire Bolsón—"or like me. In the long run, I think it best not to ask too much. I wait for knowledge to find me: I don't seek it. But you—you are a scholar. A man used to solving mysteries—yes, yes, I know, don't protest. Perhaps you can solve this one, eh?" He smiled in a way that was both ingratiating and mocking. "Perhaps you can find out what happened to Héctor Milla?"

"Why?" I asked.

"Because you are curious." He shrugged. "Because no one else wants to know."

"And if I wanted to," I said, smiling myself now, "where would I begin? You said yourself the Bolsón is endless."

He leaned toward me in the creaking straw chair. "The only point on which all the rumors agree is that both La Mascarilla and Héctor were there that night. Héctor is gone. But the witch isn't."

Two days later I was following the dry riverbed toward Las Gorgas Canyon. The day was hot, the wind silent all across the Bolsón. Piñón insects whirred softly in the air. I didn't see La Mascarilla's house until I was almost upon it, so cunningly was it tucked away in a hollow formed by the riverbed meeting the foothills of the canyon. Each time I arrived—for I made more than one visit, as it turned out—I could imagine that the house hadn't existed until an instant before and only then had been magically re-formed in expectation of my arrival. It was a small house of whitewashed clay brick with a roof of juniper and tile. The roof sagged a bit, and the walls bowed slightly. To one side a small corral enclosed four or five goats. Chickens ran around a yard loosely demarcated by a semicircle of fence wiring. A washline hung with gray underwear, cotton stockings, a dress, and a few kerchiefs ran from one window to a scraggly juniper tree, the only natural shade in the area. A few old tires with flowers inside, some oil drums, an iron stove with its door hanging open—everything in the yard seemed cast-off, abandoned, including the old woman in a brown peasant dress who sat on a bench next to the wall shaded from the sun. She was working something with her fingers—a rosary perhaps—and was soundlessly moving her lips. She didn't look up as I parked the jeep. With the engine turned off, I could hear a Beethoven piano sonata coming from a radio inside the house. The dry wind stirred and carried with it the faint smell of lemons.

As I got out of the jeep, another woman, much younger, came from behind the house. She carried a potted cactus and wore a man's faded cotton shirt and blue jeans dirty at the knees. She was about thirty-seven, tall and large-boned in a way that was unusual for inhabitants of the Bolsón, who often resembled the parched and stunted trees of their landscape. She watched me, the pot held in her hands like an offering. As I approached, I imagined I saw traces of red in the black of her hair. Her sharply incised features were more

Spanish than Indian. I was struck by the clarity of her skin, its fineness. No pore seemed visible.

"I've come to see La Mascarilla," I said. "I'm a friend of Nicanor Carreros in Fuera." The woman's eyes were the color of dark honey; the left one wandered slightly so that when she looked at me, as she was now doing, that eye seemed to be peering at something else, just off my shoulder, unseen. She put the pot on the ground and went inside without speaking. I was confused. Had I been dismissed? The Beethoven was turned down. She returned.

"That's La Mascarilla?" I asked, pointing to the old woman.

"Yes," she replied. "That is she." She ran her fingers through her hair in long, fine strokes, as if brushing it.

"You're her daughter, perhaps?"

She shook her head. "I only take care of her."

"I'd like to talk with her, if I may. I've heard much about her."

She continued to caress her hair. "What have you heard?"

"I've heard she can turn herself into a crow." I smiled, as if to say I didn't believe this.

She smiled too. "Oh, I think she can. She can also turn crows into men. Though the magic is much harder." I couldn't tell whether she was mocking me.

I looked again at the old *bruja*. Her eyes were closed, her hands still. The hem of her dress and the edges of her sleeves rippled in the hot breeze. A lizard darted from beneath her skirt and sought shelter among the bricks of the wall. She looked hard put to stand up and walk, let alone cast any sort of spell.

"I've also heard that she can make men disappear," I said.

The woman raised her brows. "Now, that would be difficult even for La Mascarilla."

I couldn't help the dramatic flourish. "I've heard that she made Héctor Milla disappear."

She seemed not at all surprised. She asked me how I had heard of Héctor Milla; I told her. I tried to appear humble, respectful. I explained I was a scholar with a sincere interest in Indian magic. I was not there to judge. From all I had heard, Héctor Milla was a deceitful man who deserved punishment. If he had received it, who was I to judge his judges?

When I finished, the woman folded her arms and rocked slightly, as if considering. Then she said, "I will tell her what you want. She may not wish to talk to you. She likes to rest in the afternoon and dream whatever she dreams. But I will tell her." She left me and walked over to the old woman. She shook her lightly. The old witch stirred like a turtle roused from its sleep in the sun. Something fluttered behind me, and I turned. Perched on one of the oil drums, not more than six feet from me, was an enormous black crow. Crows are large birds really, but this one seemed even larger than usual. It stared at me without fear.

I was startled. I looked back to the two women, then again to the crow. It was still there. It couldn't be La Mascarilla, not unless she could be in two places at once, which seemed taxing even for a great *bruja*. I shooed the crow. He didn't move. I clapped my hands, softly at first, then louder. The crow stared at me with its bright green eye. I picked up a pebble and tossed it against the oil drum. It clanged and bounced off. The crow opened its beak in a mime of cawing, though no sound came forth. Then it lazily spread its wings and flew away.

The young woman was calling to me, and I walked over.

"She will talk with you," she said. "Because you have come from so far away. But she will only speak in the old Indian language. I will translate."

Amusing, I thought.

Up close, the *bruja* seemed less substantial, as if her bulky clothing covered a stick figure beneath. Her eyes were closed, and she never once opened them to look at me. Her skin was parched and wrinkled; I had the feeling that it might crumble with a touch. Again I could smell lemons on the dry wind. I wondered how to address her. But it was she who spoke first, her words seeming to come in a single breath. She spoke in a singsong, a half-chant; she spoke as if she were recounting a tale belonging to the past and legend. The younger woman stood behind her and simultaneously translated: there had been a trial; Héctor had confessed his guilt. Antonio's family demanded immediate revenge. But the *bruja,* hating bloodshed, had interceded. She requested that Héctor's life be spared, and that she determine a fitting punishment. Antonio's family reluctantly agreed. They couldn't refuse her after all she'd done for them. And of course they were afraid of her. She should be praised, then: she had saved Héctor's life.

The old woman stopped speaking. A small dust devil raised by the wind blew through the yard. The juniper leaves rustled.

"What was Héctor's punishment?" I asked.

The *bruja* shook her head and whispered something. The young woman leaned forward to hear.

"She says that she showed him what he was."

"What does that mean?" I asked. But the old woman only shook her head and began rocking.

"Is Héctor still alive?" I persisted.

La Mascarilla would say no more. Her head fell to her chest, like a wound-down mechanical doll. Her companion sighed. "She won't say any more. She will probably be cross this evening and want extra cups of tea. Then she won't be able to sleep and will sit out here all night with the coyotes." She brushed her hair again in the gesture I now found touching. "It's not easy taking care of her. But she is all the company I have, aside from the animals."

"I'll leave then," I said. "I'm grateful for her time. Please tell her that." The woman nodded. I walked back to the jeep and drove away. A hundred yards from the house, I glanced back. The women had disappeared. A cloud passed over the sun, casting the small house into shadow, then into sunlight again as it passed on across the Bolsón. I thought of Nicanor. He would be disappointed: the mystery wouldn't be solved, at least by me.

Back in Fuera, I told him about my visit. Nicanor listened carefully. When I finished, he sighed and cracked his fingers together, one by one. He spoke solemnly. "My friend, La Mascarilla is not an old woman. La Mascarilla is the woman you were first talking with, the one with the strange eye." He laughed, the sound of a knife rubbing against stone. "She's a true witch, all right. She's already cast a spell over you."

All right, I thought as I drove back the next day. She had tricked me, and I deserved it. I had wanted to see a *"bruja"*; she had given me a *bruja,* one who even spoke in old "Indian" tongues. How they must have laughed at the *norteamericano*! I hit the steering wheel with my palm. Nicanor was right: a spell had been cast over me, but it was one I'd created. It wouldn't happen again.

When I pulled up to the house, I smelled cooking—cilantro, fat bread, beans, and garlic. I turned off the motor and waited. La Mascarilla—the real one—came to the door. With one hand she shielded her eyes from the sun, then waved to me as if I were an old friend come to dinner. She wore the same cotton shirt and blue jeans. The sun and shadows were also in the same positions as the day before. For a moment, I felt I had never left and had only dreamed of my return to Fuera. She waited in the doorway, arms folded. I couldn't help grinning as I approached. I bowed slightly.

"You lied to me," I said. "You're La Mascarilla."

I hadn't expected her to laugh, but she did, delightedly and unashamedly, a child whose not-well-kept secret has been uncovered. "Yes, yes, I am La Mascarilla. But I didn't lie to you."

"Come on." I gestured to the bench where the old woman had sat.

"That was me also," she said, still smiling.

That I didn't expect. "You were the old woman? That's what you're telling me?"

She nodded. "It's a little trick I play sometimes with strangers. A way to learn things. It's vain, I know."

"I don't believe you." The old women had been real enough, no illusion.

She shrugged. Her wandering eye seemed to glisten momentarily.

"Was the crow another of your tricks?" I asked.

"The crow?" She seemed puzzled. Then she clapped her hands and laughed. "Oh—you mean Santiago!" She whistled between her fingers like a boy, then crossed her arms and smiled. I heard the rustle of wings. The huge crow with the green eye flew from behind the house and lighted on the oil drum. It silently opened its beak. La Mascarilla lifted the lid from a small tobacco tin on the windowsill, took out a grain of corn, and put it in the bird's beak. The crow swallowed, then opened its beak again. She stroked its neck.

"See?" she said. "No magic. Just Santiago."

"He's the largest crow I've ever seen," I said. "Doesn't he ever caw?"

"He can't. He has never crowed. I found him as a small bird. He had fallen from a nest and was almost killed by dogs. To this day, he hates dogs."

Santiago preened, ignoring us.

"Why are you playing games with me?" I asked.

"I've never told you a lie," she said. "I didn't ask you to come. I don't ask you to stay." She turned her back to me and walked briskly toward the corral. The chickens followed, and so, after a moment, did I. I glanced quickly through the open door into the house, but it was too dim to see anything. The goats brayed as we approached. La Mascarilla lifted the lid from a feedbox, picked up a shovel leaning against the corral, and scooped several portions through the slats. I offered to do it for her, but she shook her head. The goats stamped and nuzzled the earth. She clucked to them. A mother goat lightly nipped the flank of its kid, sending it scampering. The chickens dashed under the slats and pecked at stray grains. Santiago flew by so close to my head that I ducked. He landed on the back of a large black goat, who didn't seem to mind.

La Mascarilla replaced the shovel against the corral and sighed. She looked almost sad. "I shouldn't do these tricks," she said. "I don't know how to conduct myself with visitors.

I have only the animals and the radio for company. Sometimes I sit up at night listening to programs from Los Angeles, Miami, Cuba, Martinique. I hear languages I don't understand from places I'll never see. These voices fill my room. Where do they really come from? They are without bodies, without souls. They are the true spirits. Now I look at you, and you are a spirit also. You appear, you disappear." She walked back toward the house, and I followed.

"You told me the truth, then, about Héctor Milla?"

"Everything I've ever told you is true."

"Then he's alive?"

"Yes."

"He's a prisoner? Somewhere?"

She shook her head. "He is free."

"Where is he?" I asked.

She stared at me in a way I hadn't seen before, her smile like a lizard surprised by the sun. "What would you give me?" she asked. "If you knew? If I told you? Would you give me your soul?"

Oh, come on, I thought. I could hear a goat snorting in the corral, the clothes flapping softly on the line, the creak of the wind through the tiles of the roof.

"Sure," I said. "Now tell me."

She grinned. "I cannot tell you anyway," she said, and glanced away. But in that glance her eyes paused momentarily on the house. If I hadn't been watching so closely, if I hadn't been expecting some signal, I might have missed it.

"I won't bother you again," I said. She nodded. When I drove away, I saw her walking back into the house, but slowly now, pained, like an old woman herself.

I asked Nicanor if La Mascarilla ever came to town. He said she did, often spending the entire day. She visited the sick and advised those with problems of the mind or heart. How did she come in? I asked. I had never seen a car or horse or donkey at her place. He shrugged. He'd never thought about it. Walked, he supposed. Or flew, I said, and we both laughed. I asked him to advise me the next time she came to town; everyone had to pass by his barbershop on the plaza. Five days later, while I was cataloging some earthen warming dishes, he knocked. La Mascarilla had been talking to his sister-in-law only an hour before; the *bruja* had told her she would be visiting the Ortiz family some distance away.

I followed the road and the riverbed back to La Mascarilla's house.

I considered the old woman: I hadn't seen her at all the last visit. Perhaps she'd been inside, or had been a visitor herself that first day. If she was there, I'd make some easy excuse.

The door was wide open, as if I'd been expected. Santiago, perched on his oil drum, opened his beak in mute greeting. I knocked once, then stepped inside. I heard a hissing sound. I waited for my eyes to adjust to the dim light. Against one wall I could see a narrow wooden bed, a crucifix above it. The figure of Christ was badly painted; thick drops of purplish blood issued from His wounds and blended with the orange of His skin. A pair of old-fashioned high-buttoned shoes stood on a straw mat beside the bed. On a nearby table her shortwave radio suddenly crackled, sputtered, and resettled into comfortable interstation hiss—the sound I'd been hearing. A small oil lamp and a book were also on the table.

The book was a text on the care and husbandry of goats, open to the chapter on birthing. One of her goats was undoubtedly pregnant. I stared at the crude illustrations of goat fetuses. Wooden wind chimes hanging by the door clacked softly, and I started. No one was there.

Shelves and cupboards constructed from cast-off wooden boxes dominated the wall opposite the bed. They contained more books, foodstuffs, bottles and jars of what appeared to be herbs, garden utensils, dishes, cheap tin silverware, neatly folded towels and blankets. A glass bottle in the shape of a hand held chocolates; a cigar box was stuffed with bits of fur and animal claws. Tacked on one side of the shelves were illustrations from badly printed religious comic books depicting episodes in the lives of the saints. Her taste seemed to run toward martyrdom—a woman identified as St. Dorothea stood engulfed in flames, a lost smile on her lips, while two angels dressed like choirboys flew about the pyre; St. Sebastian, impaled with arrows, looked toward the heavens while blood poured from his wounds in crudely drawn torrents.

A chest of drawers in the old Mission style stood against another wall. I opened a drawer: the smell of lemons was as strong as if she were in the room. But the odor that had before been subtle now seemed overripe, sickly. I shut the drawer. I felt nauseous, and had to sit on the bed. The smell of decaying lemons seemed everywhere. I held my breath, then rose and stumbled to the door, knocking the wind chimes as I passed. I grasped the clappers to silence them. Santiago, startled by my sudden exit, flapped away.

I heard a scraping behind me. I turned and blinked in the hard sunlight. Not more than fifteen feet away was a creature, come as if summoned—a naked man, walking on his hands and knees. His body was dark and crinkled from the sun and wind, and was covered with sores, many of which festered with infection. His hair was long and wildly matted; streaks of dried saliva flecked his beard. Only his eyes retained an intelligence that could perhaps remember what he had been. He stared at me, on all fours, cringing.

"Héctor," I whispered.

Hearing his name, he yelped and clawed the dirt with his knuckles, as if they were paws. Then he lowered his head to the ground and began crawling toward me on his belly, whimpering. "No," I cried. "Stay back."

I have shown him what he truly is, she had told me.

A dog.

And as I backed away from him, Santiago landed on his back and pecked him sharply. Hector howled. He arched his back and bucked, but the large crow only sank its talons deeper into his flesh and pecked again. Héctor fell to the ground and rolled in the dust, yowling.

He hates dogs to this day, she had said.

I waved my arms and backed away, but still Héctor came, whining in supplication. I could smell his odor of sweat and dust and fear, and I was sickened. He was close enough now to touch me; I was afraid he would, and that whatever demon possessed him would be transferred to me. I kicked him, I'm ashamed to say. The blow landed in his ribs. He cried out and collapsed, his breath coming in sucking sounds. Santiago flew about his head, wings beating furiously. I ran toward the jeep. Héctor struggled to his hands and feet, collapsed, then rose again. He began stumbling toward me, as best he could on all fours. I jumped in the jeep. The ignition caught and I drove away. Héctor wailed then, a wail I still hear at night within the wind. The next day I left Fuera; you might say I fled in time all the way to the Arctic Circle.

I first thought that Héctor had been drugged, possibly with jimsonweed or another powerful hallucinogen. Coupled with hypnotic suggestion, it could have driven him quite insane, to the point of believing he was a dog. But the glimmer of intelligence I thought I'd seen in his eyes... could that intelligence have known he had once been a man—and was one no longer—and thus have led him to seek the help of another man? One who, as it turned out, failed him?

I think about it constantly, and I can't decide: Was Héctor Milla really a dog, or not? Had La Mascarilla transformed him, or merely driven him mad? Is she, after all, a true witch?

The answer is important to me.

Because if she is—and she indeed let me see Héctor Milla as I had requested—she must now have my soul.

Magic

The moment she saw them, Dana wished she could fly away. They were sitting on the same side of a booth in the middle of the restaurant. Neither looked very happy. Michael was sipping a beer, and Jessica, his eight-year-old daughter, was drawing ellipses on the tabletop with her spoon. Soon they would see her: flight was impossible, invisibility her only chance. But then Michael did see her, and waved, and the hope of vanishing vanished.

Well, the show's on, Dana thought.

Michael stood up, napkin held against his lap. "Hi," Dana said. *Smile at both of them*, she reminded herself. Not really expecting a kiss, she was already sliding into the seat across from them when Michael leaned over and awkwardly grazed her cheek.

"Hi there," Dana said to the little girl with black, thick-lensed glasses who sat scrunched in the corner, half-hidden by a pile of books on the table. *Those glasses,* she thought, *make her look like a frog.* In spite of herself, Dana was disappointed: she'd fantasized that Jessica might be a beautiful child, immediately lovable, but this wasn't so.

"Jessica, this is Dana," Michael said.

"Hi," Jessica said unenthusiastically. "Daddy, can we eat now?"

"I got here as soon as I could," Dana said. *Why am I apologizing?* she wondered: Michael had wanted some time with Jessica before Dana met them for dinner. "She might be tired by late afternoon," he'd said. "It'll be good for her to have a Coke or something before you get there." It was his first Saturday with his daughter since she'd arrived from Los Angeles earlier that week, and he'd planned a busy day.

"We haven't been here too long," Michael said.

"Hours," Jessica murmured.

"Jessica—" A look passed between them, and the little girl sighed. She cocked her head from side to side, as if loosening a kink, and then began swinging her legs underneath the table.

When Michael told her a month earlier that his daughter would be coming to live with him, Dana had been incredulous. She'd been seeing Michael for five months and of course knew about Jessica, but thought of her as someone who would come only for an occasional school vacation and perhaps a month in the summer.

"You mean permanently?" she asked. "For keeps?"

"Her mother and I decided we don't want her growing up in L.A.," Michael explained. "Do you know they had a drug bust last month at her school? An elementary school? Third graders?"

"They have drugs everywhere!"

"Besides, her mother wants to move to Venice." He saw her confusion. "Venice, *California*. It's an artsy part of L.A. She's going to make rafu, or rakikki, or something."

"I thought she was a claims adjuster."

"She is. She's just starting life over. She does it every now and then."

"You start life over, you give up your child?"

"She's not giving her up—we both decided. Venice is not a good place for kids either."

"But what about us?" Dana cried.

"We'll just go on," Michael said. He hesitated. "Won't we?"

"Just like that? With a child now?"

"I know this is a surprise—"

"You bet it is, Michael. I didn't bargain for this at all."

He was silent.

"I can't believe you never asked me about this," Dana said. "You just spring this on me, and—"

"I'm sorry," Michael said.

"It's just so insensitive."

"Well, Dana, what could you have said? Really?"

"That I'm not ready for this!"

Michael took her by the shoulders. "Just give it a chance, Okay? She's a great little girl."

Dana now looked at Jessica, who sat hunched over, lips slightly parted. Behind the thick lenses her eyes were wide but unfocused, gazing at the empty space beside Dana.

As if by magic, the waitress appeared. Michael ordered the shrimp special; Jessica wanted a cheeseburger and chocolate milk.

"A cheeseburger sounds good," Dana said.

"A cheeseburger?" Michael was surprised. "For you?"

"Yes, Michael. A cheeseburger."

He shrugged.

"And a scotch too," Dana told the waitress as she collected the menus.

"I thought you didn't eat meat."

Dana glared at him.

"Well—what a day," Michael said. "We've been all over the place. Jessica, why don't you take those off the table now?" He pointed to the pile of books. "We've been to the library," he explained.

"There's no place to *put* them," Jessica complained.

"Put them between us."

"Then I won't have any room to *move*."

"Well, where are you going anyway? Come on, we're going to be eating soon."

"Here, Jessica," Dana offered. "I'll put them over here." She placed the books on the seat beside her. The one on top was *Outlaws of the Old West*.

"You're interested in cowboys, Jessica?" She held up the book. Jessica didn't reply. Dana put the book down.

"We've had a great time today," Michael said. "We went shopping and got Jessica some boots. Show Dana the boots, honey." Jessica dutifully leaned against the side of the booth and extended her leg in the air, like a ballerina at the barre.

"Very nice," Dana said.

"Then we went to the Children's Museum. They've got a great exhibition on Death there now."

"Death?" Dana blinked.

"It's to let kids get in touch with their feelings about it. So Death won't be so frightening."

"Oh."

"It was fascinating, wasn't it, honey?" Jessica nodded. "They had death masks from different cultures, and—"

"They had a mummy!" Jessica interrupted. "It was all shriveled and wrinkled—"

"There was a film that showed a dead bird—"

"—you could watch it turn yucky and then it was just bones—"

"Jessica, stop interrupting," Michael said. The little girl slumped in her seat and thrust out her lip. "It was a time-lapse photography sort of thing," he explained to Dana.

"Did you like the exhibit, Jessica?" Dana asked.

"No."

"Oh—somehow I thought you did."

"I didn't like the mouse getting eaten."

"The mouse?"

Jessica nodded. "He—"

"That was another film," Michael said. "It showed a mouse getting killed and eaten by a king snake."

"Great," Dana said.

"He swallowed it *all*," Jessica said. "His stomach blew up like a balloon." She made a grand swelling motion with her arms. "It got bigger and bigger like he was going to burst"—Dana grinned nervously—"and then he went *sploosh*!" Jessica threw her arms apart; a fine spray of saliva flew from her mouth. "Sploosh!"

"Jessica, that's not in the film at all," Michael said.

"—there were little bits of baby mouse all over, and—"

"Enough, Jessica!" The little girl giggled. A bit of spittle ran down her chin. "Come on, wipe your mouth. You're dribbling." She rubbed her face with her napkin.

"She gets this way sometimes," he said to Dana. Jessica rolled her eyes.

"I'm not sure this is such a great exhibit," Dana said.

"It teaches kids that Death is something natural. It's meant to be followed up with parental discussion." Michael took a yellow flyer from his jacket pocket. "These are suggestions for what you can talk about."

"Sploosh," Jessica murmured.

"So then you went to the library—" Dana began, but at that moment their food arrived.

"That goes there, and that goes there," Michael pointed. Dana gratefully sipped her scotch.

"Jessica loves to read," Michael said as he split open a shrimp. "Don't you, honey?"

"Can I see what else you've got here, Jessica?" Dana asked. The little girl nodded. Dana sorted through the pile, reading the titles aloud: *The Littlest Wrangler, Mrs. Lumpkin and the Twelve Angry Cats, 101 Magic Tricks for Boys and Girls, Easy Magic for Beginners*—you're interested in magic, Jessica?"

Jessica opened her cheeseburger and carefully put the pickles and tomato on the side of her plate. "Sure," she said.

"Isn't that funny? I was too when I was your age. I had a magic set with all kinds of tricks."

"Like what?"

"Well—I could make one card turn into another. And— God, I'm trying to remember—I could make a scarf disappear—"

"I never knew you were a magician," Michael grinned.

"Oh, sure. I even gave little shows in the basement for the

other kids. My mother made me a cloak, and I had a fake mustache and black hat and—"

"A real black hat?" Jessica asked.

"Well, it was cardboard, I think."

"Could you do a magic trick now?"

"Oh, I don't think so. I'm out of practice." Hidden from their view, Dana was tying a knot in one end of the cloth napkin in her lap. "Wait!" she said, as if just thinking of it. "Maybe I can." Concealing the knot in her fist, the other end hanging free, she raised the napkin for their inspection. "See?"

Dana now put the free end into her fist. "Watch," she said. She shook the napkin vigorously, once, twice, and on the third shake flung down—the knotted end. It appeared as if the napkin had knotted itself. "Da-dah!" she said triumphantly. "Magic!"

Jessica's eyes widened.

"Very good." Michael clapped. "*Very* good." He turned to Jessica. "I don't know how she did it, do you, honey?" The little girl scrunched her brow, and her glasses slipped down her nose. Dana grinned at her.

"Do it again," Jessica demanded.

"A magician never shows the same trick twice," Dana said.

"Oh, come on," Jessica pleaded. "Please!"

"Okay. Once more." Dana put the knot into her fist with the free end. "This time, why don't I make the knot disappear?" She shook the napkin as Jessica watched intently, and flung down the unknotted end.

"I know how you do it!" Jessica cried. "Daddy, she's changing them in her hand! She's throwing down the other end." Michael looked puzzled, then raised his brows.

"Ah," he said.

"Yep," Dana admitted. "You got it." She laid the napkin on the table and undid the knot.

"That's not a real trick," Jessica said.

"Well, just what would a real trick be, Jessica?" Michael asked.

"Make it disappear. You said you could make it disappear."

"A scarf," Dana said. "This is a napkin. I can't make napkins disappear."

Jessica sighed.

"I'm sorry." Dana smoothed the napkin in her lap. "I guess I'm not a real magician."

"Oh, I don't know." Michael squeezed her hand.

"Daddy, I've got to go to the bathroom." He stood up, and Jessica slid out of the booth.

"Down there," he pointed.

"Do you want me to go with you?" Dana asked.

Jessica shook her head. They watched as the little girl walked down the row of booths.

"Well," Michael said. "So."

Dana spread her hands. "Well? So?"

"So what do you think?"

"She hates me."

"Dana—what—"

"She hates me. That's all."

"Oh, Dana, come on."

"All right. She doesn't like me, then. How's that?" She took a bite of cheeseburger and put it down. "Why am I eating this? I hate cheeseburgers."

"Well, I think it's going very well for a first meeting," Michael said.

"You do, huh?"

"Dana, one meeting doesn't mean anything."

"Why do you keep calling this a meeting? I feel like I'm applying for something."

"It's not that important—that's all I'm trying to say."

Dana swirled the ice in her drink. "I don't know why you say it's not important, Michael. Of course it's important."

"Dana—just relax, okay?" He took her fingers in his hand. "There's nothing to be nervous about. It'll all work out."

"Why are you grinning all the time?"

"Grinning?"

She nodded. "It's driving me crazy. And you're really acting overbearing."

"I am?"

"Yes. To her and me both."

"Okay—I'm nervous too." He released her fingers. "I just want everybody to like each other."

"Well, maybe you should relax too." They stared solemnly at one another. Then Dana stuck out her tongue, and Michael grinned, then laughed.

"What a scene," he said.

"Yep."

"So—do you like her?"

"Sure," Dana said. "I guess. It's just—"

"What?"

"I'm not too good at this, Michael. I don't know what to say, I don't know what to do, I'm nervous—"

"Everybody's nervous. She's nervous too. It's not that she doesn't like you."

"I don't know, Michael."

He took her hand again. "She liked the magic trick," he said.

"Michael, she *hated* the magic trick. You heard her."

"She's smart." He grinned. "I didn't even figure it out the second time."

"I'm back." Jessica's voice came from somewhere below. Dana and Michael looked around the corner of the booth: Jessica was on her hands and knees on the floor.

"Jessica, get up," Michael said. "Why are you sneaking around like that?"

"I just went *poof,*" she said. He stood to let her in, and she waddled on her knees into the corner.

"I've got to go to the john too," Michael said. Dana felt a surge of panic.

"Me too," she said, rising.

"Why does *everybody* here have to go to the bathroom?" Jessica asked. Michael laughed, and then so did Dana. She sat back down.

"Go ahead," she said. "I'll keep Jessica company."

"Good." He seemed pleased.

She faced the little girl across the expanse of the booth. Jessica was swinging her legs beneath the table again.

"You're not eating any more, Jessica?"

She shook her head.

"Can I have some of your french fries?" Dana scraped them onto her plate as Jessica watched. "I love french fries."

"My mommy says they're not good for you."

"Oh, really?"

Jessica nodded.

"I don't think they're that bad," Dana said. She munched on one defiantly.

Well, what now? she wondered.

"Do you know any magic tricks, Jessica?"

Jessica shook her head.

"Maybe I can show you some sometime. Better ones. Would you like that?"

The little girl said nothing.

"I'll have to brush up," Dana said. "But I do know some other ones."

"Like what?"

"Oh, I don't know. The Mysterious Mandarin. The Five O'Clock Shadow."

Jessica looked at her doubtfully.

What's taking Michael so long? Dana wondered, and then realized that, after all, he'd just left.

"Did you like living in Los Angeles, Jessica?" she asked.

"We don't live in Los Angeles."

Dana was confused.

"We live in Alhambra," Jessica said.

Alhambra, Venice...every place in California sounded impossibly, magically far away.

"Is that near Los Angeles?" Dana asked.

Jessica shrugged.

"But your mother's moving, right? To Venice?"

Jessica slowly nodded.

"So you'll have a new place when you visit her."

"I'm going back and see her at Christmas," Jessica said.

"Ah." Dana took a deep bite of cheeseburger.

"One time I saw a magician on TV," Jessica said. "He turned a baby bird into an alligator."

"Wow."

"It was just a baby alligator."

"That's some trick."

"Are you going to marry my daddy?"

Dana was startled. "I—I don't know," she said, and then, "Maybe." Almost apologetically, she added, "We like each other a lot."

"If you and Daddy got married, you still wouldn't be my real mother," Jessica said softly, not looking at her.

"No—of course not, honey. I—"

"—because my real mommy is in California."

"Of course she is, Jessica. I'd never take the place of her."

"You'd never be my real mommy," Jessica repeated.

"Jessica—I don't *want* to be your real mommy."

The little girl stared into her lap.

"Your father and I don't even know if we'll get married," Dana said. "I don't know. Maybe we won't. Maybe—"

"Even if she died, you wouldn't be my real mommy."

"Jessica, what are you talking about? She's not going to die."

"I wish she'd die," Jessica said, her eyes glistening behind the thick lenses of her glasses. "I wish she'd die, and he'd die, and—" Then she was crying, and trying hard not to.

"Jessica—look—oh Jesus—" Dana rummaged in her purse for a tissue, but couldn't find one. "Here," she said, offering Jessica her napkin. "Come on, take it." The little girl accepted the napkin, but just held it in her hand. "Wipe your eyes, okay? You don't want your father to see you crying, do you?"

Jessica took off her glasses and dabbed her eyes. She squinted at Dana.

Poor little thing, Dana thought, *she can hardly see at all.* She dipped her napkin in her water glass. "Here, lean over," she said. Jessica's chin was hot in her palm as Dana gently rubbed her face.

"There," she said. Jessica quickly drew back across the

table, but the warm imprint of the child's face remained on Dana's hand.

"I saw you talking to her," Michael said later. "That's good." It had still been light when they left the restaurant, the spring evening chilly and sweet, and they'd decided to walk through the park. Jessica ran ahead of them, in and out of the lengthening shadows.

"No," Dana said. "It's not."

"What do you mean?"

She hesitated. "Michael, maybe I should just disappear for a while. Maybe that's the best thing."

He stopped. "Why?"

"She's upset about coming here, she misses her mother—I mean, it's everything. It's just not the right time now."

He stuffed his hands in his pockets.

"So maybe we should just cool it awhile—"

"I don't want that," he said.

"Well, maybe it's best."

"You just want to take off? Fly away?"

"Michael—she doesn't want me. At least for now."

"How do you—"

"And I'm not sure I want her."

He blinked.

"You've got to grant me that, Michael," she said. "I just don't know."

"So you don't like her."

Dana thought for a moment. "No, I do like her. Even if she doesn't like me."

"I wish you'd quit saying that."

"It's just that I'm not sure I'm ready for all this, Michael."

"You've got to give it time," he said. "Things don't just happen overnight"—he snapped his fingers—"like magic."

"They should," Dana murmured.

They began walking again and crossed the bridge by the duck pond. On the other side, Jessica squatted by the edge and peered intently into the water.

"Something really should be done about those glasses of hers," Dana said. "Contacts maybe. She probably feels so self-conscious."

"You think so?"

Dana nodded. "I hated my glasses when I was a kid."

"She's never said anything."

"Michael—she probably doesn't even know about contacts." She watched as Jessica trailed her fingers back and forth through the water.

"You know," Dana said, "the funny thing is she looks enough like me to actually be my daughter."

"Really? You think so?"

"Yes, I do. Isn't that funny? Somebody could look at us and think we were just a regular family, out for a walk."

Jessica rose and walked along the bank, hands stuffed in her pockets like her father.

"You know what really upset me?" Dana said. "When she said it wasn't a real trick. Remember?"

He nodded.

"That really upset me. Isn't that strange?"

Michael put his arm around her shoulders. "Do you want to stay with me tonight?"

"Michael—we just talked about that!"

"Oh, come on," he grinned. "Take a chance."

"What about Jessica?"

"She knows we stay together. I told her you might stay over."

"I don't know if that was so smart, Michael. I mean, the first time she meets me?"

He sighed. "Okay, maybe you're right."

They walked a little farther without speaking. Frogs were croaking from the pond, and the trees seemed to bend over, as if listening.

"Okay," Dana said. "I'll stay. But I'll leave before she gets up."

Michael laughed. "That's a switch, isn't it? The woman leaving early?"

"Modern times," Dana said.

Dana slept fitfully, and each time she awoke, was aware that she and Michael were not alone. Down the hall, in another room, Jessica was sleeping. *I wonder if she'll wake up and come in,* Dana thought. She remembered how as a child she'd awaken in a silent house and feel certain her parents had left her. She'd go to their room and stand by the bed, just to reassure herself that they were still there.

Restless, Dana got up and opened a window. The night had strangely changed, become warm and balmy, almost like summer. She looked beyond the yard to the blackness of the sky and stars. A warm night wind poured around and through her, quickening her, making her shine. Dana touched her breasts, her arms. Anything seemed possible.

Magic, she thought.

And then a strange idea came to her: she would go see

Jessica. No sooner had she thought it than she was there, standing beside the little girl's bed. Jessica's knees were pulled to her chest and her brow was furrowed, lip thrust forward, defiant even in sleep.

Dana shook her lightly. Instantly she was awake, eyes wide. Dana put a finger to her lips.

"I want to show you something," she whispered. Jessica threw off the sheet and began to follow her, then stopped. "My glasses," she said. She put them on, and Dana had to smile, the little girl looked so much like a small blinking owl. They went downstairs into the backyard. The air was electric, green, humming.

"Stay here," Dana ordered. She walked to the center of the yard and turned to face Jessica. The little girl crossed her arms, waiting.

"I want to show you a real trick," Dana said.

She closed her eyes, spread her arms, and slowly rose until she was hovering a few feet above the ground. Jessica gasped, then was silent, struck dumb. Dana continued to rise. *So easy,* she thought. When she was some twenty feet high, she tucked herself into a ball and tumbled over and over through the air, from one end of the yard to the other and back again to the center. Jessica watched, openmouthed. Unfolding herself, Dana stretched lengthwise, as if swimming, and flutter-kicked through the shimmering air. Jessica clapped. Encouraged, smiling now, Dana sat as if riding an invisible unicycle. Crossing her arms like a Cossack, she pedaled through the air, whirling and twirling and backpedaling above Jessica's head, all the while making tooting sounds. The little girl squealed with delight. It was good to see her laugh; Dana was enjoying herself immensely. *This is what a real magician does*, she thought with satisfaction. It wasn't hard at all. She hadn't even had to practice—she'd been ready all the time.

Dana finished with a series of grand midair somersaults, each larger than the one before. Then, as Jessica applauded fervently, she put her hands over her head and slowly descended, toes first, onto the ground.

"I just wanted to show you I could do this," she told Jessica. "I wanted to show you this was possible."

"Can you show me?" Jessica asked breathlessly.

Dana smiled. "I don't know. A real magician doesn't give away her secrets."

"But *could* you?"

"Maybe. But not right away. In time."

Jessica nodded solemnly. Dana held out her hand, Jessica took it, and once more they were back in the little girl's room.

"One thing," Dana whispered as she tucked Jessica in bed. "Let's not tell your father."

"No," Jessica agreed.

"He wouldn't understand."

Jessica nodded.

"It'll be our secret," Dana said. "Here, let's take off your glasses." She placed them on the table beside the bed. Jessica grasped Dana's hand.

"I want to tell you a secret," she said. Dana leaned closer. The little girl's breath was warm and milky against her ear.

"Jessica's not my real name."

"Oh? What is it, then?"

"Jesse."

"Jesse?"

"Like Jesse James."

"Jesse." Dana kissed her. "I'll remember."

And then she was again in bed beside Michael and was once more tumbling through an ether, this one much darker and heavier, making her sleep. It seemed very important to remember everything, and then she realized why: she must remember because even by tomorrow Jessica—Jesse—might have forgotten. She was a child, after all, and children's memories are short. *But I can remember,* Dana thought, *and be there to remind her*—that was also what a real magician did, almost as a real mother might, one who believed in magic and could bring them safely, if not speedily, home.

Elias Schneebaum

When Elias Schneebaum was a student at Latin Day School in 1928, he wrote several hymns in the Protestant style for the chapel choir, as well as a new setting for the school song—not the *alma mater,* which had been based upon a melody by Buxtehude and hardly needed amending, but the one sung on informal occasions by the Glee Club. While at Harvard he commuted once a week to New York to study composition with Lucian Ferre, who had himself studied with Nadia Boulanger, whose photograph hung on Ferre's wall next to a Nigerian canoe mask. He told Elias marvelous anecdotes about "Madame": she was fond of walnut tortes dipped in honey and would nibble them throughout a session while Ferre salivated; she suffered from poor circulation and in winter would often sit on a hot water bottle which was periodically refilled from a kettle kept simmering on the stove. Elias told Ferre that he would like to study with

Boulanger. Could he possibly write her a letter on his behalf? His teacher said he would. Some months later, when Elias asked if he had received any word, Ferre said that Madame had replied that she could accept no more students. Elias took this with good cheer and decided to go to Paris anyway. He obtained a room above a Greek sweet shop, outside of which old men sat at a long table drinking small cups of coffee and chattering in singsong voices throughout the day. Later that week he called on Madame Boulanger at her apartment on the second floor of a yellow plaster building near the Val-de-Grâce. A woman of some age, not Madame, answered the door.

"My God, another American," she exclaimed.

Elias, flustered, began explaining in bad French that he was a composer and wished to see Madame Boulanger.

"One does not call on Madame Boulanger just like this," the woman said tartly.

"I'm sorry," Elias said.

"It's just not done." The woman squared her back.

"I'm sorry," Elias repeated. Not realizing he was supposed to leave, Elias didn't; the woman, too polite to close the door on his face, waited. They stared at one another.

"Well, you *are* an American," she sighed, as if to explain how Elias could still be standing there. Sensing a softening of heart, he quickly explained about Lucian Ferre's letter. He understood that Madame could take no new students, but perhaps he could at least show her a few of his compositions? The woman replied that if he sent them to the flat in the next day or so, along with a proper note, she would see they were delivered to Madame Boulanger. Elias did so, and some weeks later received a short reply in a fine spidery hand. Nadia

Boulanger could not recall any letter from Lucian Ferre, whom she only vaguely remembered, but it was true nevertheless that she could not accept any new students. No mention was made of Elias's compositions, and he never returned to pick them up.

For a time Elias would stroll by the yellow building, pausing beneath the second-floor window. One time he heard a piano. It was a spring day and the tall, green-shuttered windows were open to the sky. A pot of geraniums was artfully balanced on the balcony railing. A black cat sat counterpoised on the opposite railing, its haunches hanging precariously over the edge. The unseen pianist played a diatonic scale once, twice, then again, each time in a different rhythm. Then the same scale was played as asymmetric chords. Finally the pianist broke into quick, nervous jazz phrasings. Then silence. When Elias passed by on his return some hours later, the window was closed, the geraniums brought in, the cat gone. It was not that important to study with Nadia Boulanger, he decided.

It seemed that Paris was always overcast that year, a fine mist tracing webs across Elias's face as he walked in the evening. He watched the crowds on Saturday mornings looking for bargains among the outdoor clothes racks on the Rue de Rivoli; he walked along the Quai de Gesvres and saw a woman emerge from an old vegetable barge with two small orange birds—finches, he thought—and throw them up into the sky. They rose like a perfect thought, bisecting the Tour St.-Jacques in their flight. He spent many afternoons—all of them remembered as Thursday and rainy—in the Museum of the Hôtel de Cluny, wandering among its collection of Medievalia. In its center was a small Gothic chapel, formerly

an abbots' oratory, with a stairway that led to a lower garden.
It was here he toyed with the idea of becoming Catholic. It
was here, too, that he embraced and kissed Lucie, and considered asking her to marry him. She was a set designer for
the Théâtre Steinfels; they had met one morning while watching a red and yellow hot-air balloon advertising Gryphon
cigarettes rise from behind the buildings on the Rue du Four.
Lucie giggled when he kissed her, then glanced toward the
chapel entrance. They both laughed at their indiscretion, and
the moment of asking her passed.

Lucie never pressed for any declaration of love, however.
She would shake her closely cut blond hair, which she at-
tempted to keep in curls with a hot iron and foul-smelling
lotions, and tell Elias about the latest intrigues at the Théâtre
Steinfels. It was always in financial and political difficulties.
A right-wing faction was about to take over the company,
which was run by Monsieur Steinfels along the lines of a
socialist commune, with shares divided among the members.
It was a great experiment in political theater, Lucie said. Elias
thought the plays boring, and after seeing two, refused to go
anymore. Lucie called him a *tête de cochon* and had refused
to see him for some weeks. Eventually the theater went bank-
rupt, although not before being closed by the police. It seemed
that the material for the painted backdrops for Steinfels's
production of *Polyeucte* in modern dress had been stolen from
a factory in Fontainebleau. Gilles-Roy, the chief set designer,
protested that he had bought the material in good faith from
an Algerian source, which he refused to name. Steinfels, portly
in his indignation, slapped Gilles-Roy, called him an assassin
of art, and was in turn arrested. The police confiscated the
material even though the scenery had already been painted

and appliquéd. Lucie suspected that the sale of the contraband
material had been set up by the theater's right-wing faction.
"I won't work with those fascists," she protested, and re-
signed—a wasted gesture, as it turned out, since the theater
never reopened. After that she spent much of her day at cafés,
talking with other unemployed friends about starting new
companies. Ideas and projects rose as grandly as the Gryphon
balloon. Elias often joined her in the afternoons. Lucie lit one
cigarette from the butt of another and told him of the celeb-
rities she had seen. Marcel Thil, then at the height of his
boxing prowess, once walked by with a woman on either
arm. Another time she saw Julien Green drinking *doubles*
with three friends. He had banged his knee against the sharp
metallic table edge when he rose to go.

"Without paying, of course," she said. "He yowled like a
little monkey."

Elias thought of committing suicide twice that year. The
first time was when he discovered Lucie had been unfaithful
to him, not once but several times. "So American," Lucie
sighed as he sat at the table, clasping and unclasping his
hands.

"What? To kill myself?" he asked.

"No. To threaten it when you don't mean it. You have no
guile."

Elias had to laugh at that, and so Lucie's infidelities became
another thing he came to accept in the course of a generally
satisfactory life in Paris.

But suicidal thoughts came in pairs. Some months after
this, Elias decided he would never be a true composer and
subsequently fell into a deep depression. Life, which had
seemed full of measured pleasures, stretched before him like

a deserted street. That was his dream, in fact, of those weeks:
an empty street in autumn in no particular city, a few leaves
falling from an unseen tree, distant music from a parade that
has just turned the corner. A woman comes out of a doorway
and throws a pail of water on the pavement. The water in-
creases in speed and volume across the rough stones until it
is a briny torrent heading straight for Elias. If it touches him—
if even the smallest drop touches him—he will dissolve. He
is afraid, and cannot move. Elias awakens and is wet indeed
from his own sweat.

Again he contemplated suicide, but decided to give up com-
posing instead. It was less trouble, even if no less final. The
dream of the empty street ceased. He no longer walked by
Nadia Boulanger's apartment, and its yellow walls and green
shutters became in time the fabric of other dreams.

"What will you do now that you're no longer a composer?"
Gérard asked. Gérard was a playwright Elias had met through
Lucie. At age thirty-eight he had had a single one-act play
produced at a small theater in the Marais.

"I'll return to New York," Elias said.

"Fortunately, you have no money worries," Gérard reminded him, as he did quite often. "Your inheritance." Gérard
had a thin wife who never ate or drank when she accompanied
him to the cafés. He also had three children, one of whom,
Lucie told Elias, suffered from a congenital spinal defect and
was rumored to be dying: his rib cage was gradually crushing
his lungs, smothering him from within. Gérard was interested
in the spiritual world. He and Elias would walk along the
Rue Monge—the rich smell of the Seine as fragrant as plowed
earth—and Gérard would discourse on the early Christian
mystics, the Sufi masters, the rabbis of the Kabala. He told

Elias that Time was not linear, binding the phenomenal world to simple cause and effect; rather, it was coeternal. All Time existed in any one moment of time, if only we had power to apprehend it—a state of grace reserved for the most exalted mystics.

"I, for example, am both here with you"—he tapped Elias on the shoulder—"and also dead. And not yet born. If not yet born, or dead, then I am someone else at this moment, or somewhere else."

"It makes my head swim," Elias said.

"Exactly."

One day they learned that the café would no longer be serving *kirsch*. It was the first indication to Elias that relations between France and Germany were strained. Soon rumors of war were all anyone did hear in the cafés. The night Elias left Paris, he wrote Gérard a check which he knew represented more than his friend had earned in the past eight months. Gérard thanked him and said he would write. In turn he gave Elias his personal copy of *Les Idées philosophiques et religieuses de Philon d'Alexandrie*. They all came to the Gare du Nord for Elias's departure—Gérard, his wife, Lucie. Elias had a bad head cold which the fumes and noise did little to palliate. Slightly feverish, he accepted a small bouquet of yellow roses from Lucie, who cried and kissed him repeatedly. She would write, too, she said. She called him "my little American," which she had never done before. "I will come to you," she told him. "I will come see you in America." The train pulled out of the station, and Elias turned at what he thought was the appropriate dramatic moment to wave good-bye, but discovered that he was facing in the wrong direction, having somehow disoriented himself. By the time he crossed the aisle,

Gérard and Lucie were already walking up the platform, ever smaller figures in the pale smoke of his fast-approaching past.

Elias Schneebaum, no longer composer, returned to New York and let a small apartment in the West Eighties with a view of Central Park. He spent most of his afternoons at the Public Library reading the works of Vedanta masters Gérard had recommended in preparation for a trip to India. Then came the War. At first Elias regretted not being able to make his pilgrimage, but then reflected that it probably made little difference in the curve of his life. We are the same person, regardless, he wrote to Gérard, not certain whether the letter would reach him. He looked out the window to Central Park, braided with thin smoke from skaters' fires. All things will surely end equally, he wrote again. He touched the cold pane of glass and was rewarded with a shiver.

After the War he again received letters from Lucie and Gérard. Interestingly enough, Lucie became more faithful in correspondence than she ever had been in love. She wrote that the War had been a "great inconvenience." She was now owner of a small pâtisserie near Elias's old apartment. Elias wondered where she had gotten the money to invest in a business, something not only improbable for Lucie but also antithetical to her political principles as he had known them. She sent him a photograph, cropped to remove whoever stood by her side. She was standing on a bridge, the hand of her unknown companion resting on the stone balustrade next to her elbow. She looked well. He hair was cut the same, although her dress was longer, more modish. For some years afterward she would send him photographs. She stood on bridges, in streets, beside statues in parks. Her hair did change styles, and once—although it was hard to tell in the black-

and-white photograph—he thought it changed color. In the last photo she sent, she wore hiking boots and knickers, as if she had become a Tyrolean guide. Elias was amused. Then she stopped sending them. "You are past the age for souvenirs," she wrote. "You are at the age where memory alone must do." Much later, the letters themselves stopped. Elias imagined her growing ever more plump and content in a flat that was too warm in winter, too stuffy in summer. He tried to imagine her becoming gray, as he was, but the yellow of her curls held too strong a grip on his memory.

Gérard wrote also—short, carping letters whose script ran up the page from left to right. The paper was always thick and poorly dyed. Things had gone badly during the War, he wrote. His wife had died, which puzzled him, since he had always assumed their son would die, but he grew healthier each year. His spine was miraculously straightening itself. He was the subject of two medical papers, and was often exhibited at hospitals in Paris, for which Gérard received small honorariums. He had given up playwrighting: "I realized one day that my life itself was a bad dream. How could I construct a fantasy greater than that? Living was the best play of all." He now worked as a proofreader in a company publishing religious manuals for the Cistercian Order. Occasionally he allowed some particularly sacrilegious or scatological typographical error to slip by.

"The thing that is most abhorrent," he wrote, "is not the abysmal thinking, the religious fervor approaching idolatry, but the *style*. When the intellect declines, style falters first. There has never been a bad thinker who was a good writer. Name me one! Of course, the best thinkers have not written at all: I'm thinking of Jesus, Socrates, Buddha. But among mortals, a great religious man is also a great writer. Thomas Aquinas. St. Augustine. Dante, certainly. I don't know what I'm saying, really. It is late evening, my eyes, the work, the execrable work."

Elias was now living in Connecticut in a great stone mill-house he had bought with the remainder of his father's inheritance. When he had first seen the house, he had touched its whitewashed walls and felt the coolness, the slight moistness of the stone. He felt secure, bounded. Nothing would be asked of him here. The house sat at the end of a long rising lawn at whose other end was a small lake with woods surrounding. "Why do you want to live in the forest?" his mother had asked. "It makes it hard to visit." She had visited him only once when he lived sixteen blocks away in the city. "I'll keep a pied-à-terre here," he assured her, and did so for a time, thinking of it as a studio to which he could repair if he ever chose to compose again. After three years, he gave it up, having stayed in it only twice. He was quite content in his stone house in the country. On winter evenings, the lawn sleeping under snow and the trees bare to the sky, he sat in front of the fireplace reading Eastern philosophy, Simenon mysteries, music journals. He spent one entire winter reading the late Hellenistic mystics and the poetry of Thomas Traherne. Another winter he stopped using electric lights, preferring to read by the light of kerosene lanterns. Electric lamps were reserved for guests. When he shaved at night (he always shaved before going to bed, rather than in the morning), the leathery glow of the lantern transformed his face to that of an Eskimo, a medieval tetherman, an Ecuadorian shepherd.

In spring when the smell of clover filled the lawn, he walked through the woods with Charles, a dachshund he had ob-

tained for company. Elias parted the tall ferns with a walking
stick while Charles trotted carefully behind. His first summer
in the house, Elias found an abandoned beaver dam across
a small creek that fed the lake. The dam had broken on one
side, and water poured through. The caked mud, leaves, and
sticks were settling slowly to ruin. Sitting on a log by the
dam, Elias was certain he had lived forever. This present life
was only the latest—and perhaps the most useless—in a
series that stretched through time like an endless dream. The
idea was not new to Elias, but was now perceived with all
the force of personal truth. He was gripped with a passion
he hadn't felt for years. He carried Charles back home, the
little dog whimpering with delight, and made himself a pot
of tea.

He wrote of this experience to Gérard, who replied that
while mystical experiences of a reincarnative nature were
common, they were not to be trusted. They were nothing
more than the repetitive manifestations of one's psyche staring
at itself, its image reflected as a series of images distorted into
other faces, much as one sees oneself many times over when
looking into two opposing mirrors. There was a certain paradox here, he said, but not enough of one to worry over.
(Elias failed to see the paradox, but thought better than to
ask. Gérard was not a happy man, he knew.) The unity of
the soul, Gérard continued, was the basis of all Western re-
ligions and should be respected. He was through with Eastern
philosophy, anyhow. He advised Elias that he was taking
instruction in Judaism.

"I have met a woman," he wrote, "a Jewish widow from
Corsica. She is quite firm in her belief. Before she will marry
me, she insists I convert. She has a child who is pure peasant,

Jew or not. He glares at me. I swear he is muttering curses and giving me the Evil Eye. They are all old Catholic peasants, these Corsicans, even the Jews. But they're not too bad, the lessons that is. I believe Judaism was meant for me. The rabbi is young, from Budapest, and we argue. He says that if God wanted to put himself into a little box he could do it, whereas I say that the very idea violates the concept of God as omnipresent. But—he says—then you are denying that God is all-powerful unto Himself. You are saying He is bounded by a human idea of size. But—I say—what if that idea were not man's, but God's? And so it goes. It passes the time.

"I am becoming a peasant in my old age, *cher* Elias. I am fortifying myself with rabbis and peasant women. Everyone in his life reaches a turning, don't you think? A door is shut, so softly you don't hear it. What room does it close? The dreams of youth? of love? You only know that the past is past, and the future too belongs to that past. Anyway, this reincarnation of yours: be careful. *Sois honnête.* The labyrinth of the Self is the only one that requires you to weave the same thread that will guide you out."

Some time after this letter, Elias received an announcement printed on heavy blue paper. Gérard had married a Madame Claude Rinelli. Written at the bottom was "All is now to see." Elias had not heard from Gérard since.

But one night a few years later, Elias awoke, certain someone was in the room watching him. Charles slept soundly at the foot of the bed. Elias heard sighing from one corner, the sighing of one who has given up the struggle to live, yet lives on and is the sadder for it. He fumbled for the matches by the lantern, but couldn't find them. Elias was frightened for the first time since he was a child; like a child, he pulled the covers over his head. The sighing intensified, and then became a warm wind that smelled of pepper and cloves, funereal spices. It passed through the sheets and through Elias himself. He burned with its dry heat. Then it was gone. He uncovered himself. Charles was still asleep; it was now first light. He was certain that Gérard had died. Elias didn't write again, and since he heard nothing further from his old friend, assumed this was so.

His mother died, reluctantly. With part of her inheritance, Elias built a large reflecting pool in the side yard and surrounded it with hedges. He had a tiny swan boat made, no bigger than a washtub, and fitted an umbrella over it. Occasionally he would float in it to the middle of the pool and pass the afternoon reading.

He joined the local chapter of the Theosophical Society and began studying texts by Schelling, Böhme, and Blavatsky. He often sat reading by the fireplace in the kitchen, brandy in hand, Mozart on the phonograph. The fire cast a soft glow over the roughly textured pages so that the words seemed scribed, not printed. He imagined himself a monk bent over a text in his cell—a cell which resembled the tiny chapel in the Cluny. One night Elias realized that that was exactly what he was—a solitary, celibate man poring over a text by candlelight in a cold stone building. He laughed. *Perhaps I was meant for spiritual matters after all,* he thought. The woods surrounding the house seemed to sigh and move closer. The telephone rang. He picked it up, but no one was on the line, only static that softened into a murmur like a faraway sea. This began to happen often. Several times Elias thought he heard music behind the static, though of what shape or tone or form he couldn't tell—only that it had the symmetry of music, not noise. He was not at all frightened by these mysterious ringings. He felt them benevolent, as most things in his life had been benevolent. At Theosophical Society meetings when debate centered about the nature of Evil—whether it derived from Man or from archonistic forces beyond Man— Elias dozed, and thought of himself cutting radishes for a salad on a rainy morning.

Sometimes he had trouble sleeping though, and would awaken in the bluish vacuum of night expecting to find himself transformed. The possibility of this transformation being either marvelous or monstrous made him shiver. He half expected to touch his skin and find horny rind, or to open his mouth and make only small croaks or chirps. He lay in bed listening to the leaves dropping like butterflies on the roof. He was certain that if he opened his window he would see the elder trees that bordered the lake silently marching away. Where do they go? Elias wondered. What do they dream of? Charles would moan by the foot of the bed, lost in a dream of his own. The house turned in its old stone sleep.

One evening it was his turn to host the society's monthly meeting. Elias prepared small quiches with lemon butter during the afternoon while the sky darkened and distant thunder rumbled. As his guests arrived, the air turned as golden as a Venetian painting. Lightning flashed over the lake.

"Lightning in evening is almost green, isn't it?" Dr. Casen, the president of the Society, said. Elias was walking with him and Gloria Talbert to the beaver dam, which they had insisted on seeing. Gloria was in her early fifties, with blond hair that wanted to curl, but which she kept brushed straight and long. Still trim, she had the quiet good looks of a woman comfortable with—but not needing—fine linen and crushed ice.

She had moved here recently from somewhere farther north. Her husband had died, or left her; Elias had forgotten which. He liked her, and she seemed to like him, although lately he had felt her listening to him more attentively than what his words warranted. When she had asked to see his "famous beaver dam," he had invited Dr. Casen along too.

Water trickled over the silent dam. Charles rooted in a bed of moss near a rotting maple. Elias glanced at Gloria, whose blond hair was streaked with red from the sunset light falling through the trees. Dr. Casen poked at the dam and grunted.

"Where are the beavers?" Gloria asked, craning her neck like a child. "Did we scare them away?"

"No. It's abandoned," Elias said.

"I don't think they build dams anymore," Dr. Casen said. He worked his jaw slowly, as if chewing the thought. "I used to see plenty of them near Stonington, where I grew up. Never saw a beaver, though." He continued poking at the dam with his stick. "These things last forever."

"They're such cute animals," Gloria said. "It's a shame they're gone. Why do you suppose they left, Elias?"

"Disease is a possibility," Dr. Casen said before Elias could speak. "An animal population in close proximity could be wiped out fairly quickly."

"Maybe they just got frightened," Elias said. "Maybe when they built the house so close, they got scared and moved on."

Charles snorted and jumped away from where he had been rooting, surprised by something in the moss.

"Charles!" Gloria laughed, scooping the dachshund up in her arms. Charles moaned and let his head fall back. She tickled his belly and let him down, and he waddled off toward the house.

"It's amazing to put that much effort into something and then just leave it," Dr. Casen said, taking a last look at the dam as they walked back. Gloria took Elias's arm; he was conscious of the light pressure of her fingers through his sleeve. Thunder rumbled across the lawn, and Elias noted that the clouds had moved closer. Through the bay windows he could see Arch Wainrey arranging chairs for the meeting.

"Have you ever been tempted by a great temptation?" Gloria asked.

"Oh, once or twice," Elias said. He tried to think when, then remembered the small chapel in the Cluny where he had kissed Lucie and considered asking her to marry him.

"Did you give in?"

"Of course," he lied.

They walked in silence up the lawn.

"I'd be lonely here," Gloria said. "Don't you find it lonely?"

"No, not really," Elias replied. "I don't need much. I'm an old monk at heart."

"You're a saint," she laughed, and released his arm. She said it in a way that so reminded him of Lucie that for a moment Elias felt suspended between two times—the past and the present-in-the-past.

The evening's speaker came from the Boston chapter and was a printer by trade: he told Elias that his doorknocker resembled an old Germanic colophon. His talk concerned a community of first-century Jewish monks (which surprised Elias, who had no idea there ever had been Jewish monks) called the Therapeutae, who lived in Egypt near Lake Mareotis. They devoted their days to silence and prayer, talking only at the Sabbath meal, when they argued text and doctrine. The monastery reputedly possessed one of the largest libraries of philosophic and religious works outside of Alexandria. In the second century the Therapeutae were ordered disbanded by the Roman governor under pressure (it was suspected) from the Dividae, a rival religious sect. The monks took a last ritual meal together and then committed mass suicide by throwing themselves off the cliffs above the lake. The monastery was turned into a garrison for Roman troops, its library transported to the governor's palace and thence to Rome. It found its way into the hands of a wealthy government functionary who in turn sold it to a syndicate of scholars. After the fall of Rome, it vanished from history, although some accounts claim it was taken, in whole or in part, to the Irish abbey of Glenhoven, which was itself destroyed by fire in the early ninth century.

After his lecture the printer told Elias that he had seen the library through astral projection: it existed intact in the cellar of a large country estate somewhere in the valley of the Rhône. He had no idea who owned the country house, since he had never been able to project himself above the cellar. But he assumed the proprietor to be a scholar of some kind: a scroll had been open on a worktable and a translation to French begun. The printer had been able to project himself there only twice, the second time some four months after the first. Little had changed: the translation had progressed a few pages, a dictionary of Greek lexicon now lay beside it. An armchair had replaced the Gothic chair at the worktable. The ashes were still warm in the small fireplace in the corner. The library's owner had probably just left, having worked late into the night and gone to bed with the early morning just as the Boston printer, on his side of the world, began his astral journey.

Elias offered to drive him to the train station, but Emma Thornton overheard and volunteered to do it instead. The station was only four miles from her house, she reminded Elias. The printer's departure seemed to signal an end to the evening. A warm wind was blowing as Elias shook hands by the door. The elder trees by the garden lowered their heads in anticipation of the rain. Elias heard drops among the overhead leaves, although none yet reached the ground. He stood by the bay window overlooking the lawn and saw a figure silhouetted against the lake, whether man or woman he couldn't tell. It didn't move, although he knew it was watching him. He waved, and in shocking synchronicity it waved back. Elias's arm fell limply to his side.

"Ghosts," he whispered.

Then the figure was walking up the lawn toward him. When it passed under the garden lights, he saw it was Gloria. He thought she had left with Dr. Casen.

"I saw you watching me," she said. "I tried to stay very still and pretend I didn't know."

"I thought you were a ghost," Elias said.

"It's a lovely evening," Gloria sighed. "It smells like mint and magnolias. And rain." She took his arm. They walked around the side of the house to her car, which had been obscured by the large linden tree.

"I thought you were a ghost," Elias said again. "Isn't that strange?"

"It's because of that spooky speaker," Gloria said. "I don't know where Casen is getting them from these days. I liked it when we had discussions about selections we read. They were more—edifying. These people take things so seriously." She breathed deeply of the evening air. "You must be terribly happy living here. This house. The lake. That little pool. It's all so calm and beautiful. A perfect jewel."

"I think I've been happy," he said. "All in all."

They stood by her car. "Do you need any help cleaning up?" Gloria asked. "The dishes?"

"No. You're kind."

"I've been meaning to ask you—whatever do you do with that little boat at the pool? It's such a funny little thing. Do you actually use it?"

"Yes," Elias said. "Sometimes I go out into the middle of the pool and just sit. When the water settles and the clouds are reflected in the pool it's as if I'm suspended in nothingness."

"It sounds lovely," Gloria said. "I must come out and try it sometime."

Elias tried to open the car door, but it was locked. Gloria searched in her purse for the keys. "I know it's silly to lock the door here," she said. "Force of habit." She found the keys and unlocked the door. Elias opened it for her. She hesitated before getting in.

"I could be very happy here," she said. She touched his arm. "If it were mine, I mean. If I lived here." She shook her head and laughed. "I mean, if I were you."

The phone rang. Gloria kissed him lightly on the cheek. "Your phone's ringing," she said, and got in the car. Elias closed the door.

"It'll stop," he said as she pulled away.

Elias didn't bother to answer it when he got inside, and it did stop. He picked up cups from the living room and stacked them in the sink with the plates. He would wash dishes in the morning. He emptied the coffee urn and filled it with baking soda and water. Charles came into the kitchen, sniffed at his food bowl—empty now—and whined to go outside. Elias opened the kitchen door and the little dog disappeared into the night.

As Elias undressed and folded his clothes on the valet rack, a thunderclap burst overhead with such intensity that the house trembled. The rain that had been threatening all evening immediately followed. Elias moved from room to room to make sure all the windows were shut. In each room the rain sounded differently: in one it was like pennies in a coin box Elias had had as a child; in another, like blows on a hollow log drum. It was music of a sort, he thought. He hummed a tune he had composed in Paris and had forgotten until now. Then he brushed his teeth, gargled with soda water, and sat on the edge of the bed. The electricity dimmed, came back.

Charles, he remembered, and walked downstairs to the kitchen door, expecting to see the little dog under the porch light. But Charles wasn't there. He called into the glistening curtain of rain, but heard no response. He closed the door. Charles—most likely frightened by the storm—was probably hiding under the house, he thought. Elias turned off the porch light and went back upstairs. He stood by the bedroom window for a while staring into the rain. Another loud thunderclap, and lightning—the acrid smell of ozone wove a circle around the house. The lights dimmed again, and this time went out for good. Elias thought about lighting the kerosene lantern, then decided not to bother. He told himself that Charles was safe: no predators would be prowling tonight. Elias lay back on his pillow and closed his eyes. Beneath the steady pulsing of the rain, the house seemed to be breathing.

He awoke. The lights were on. For a moment Elias panicked, thinking someone was in the room until he remembered that the storm had knocked them out. Power had been restored. The rain had stopped, although it still dripped thickly from the trees. Elias had no idea how long he'd been asleep.

He heard a sound, low and keening. He went over to the window and looked into the night. Clouds moved around the moon like hobgoblins, casting quick shadows among the trees. But he saw nothing on the moonlit lawn. Then Elias heard it again, a call almost; and when he looked down the lawn toward the lake, he saw her in almost the same place Gloria had stood before. Her face was lost in the shadows, but the shape of her body, the tilt of her head, was unmistakable, as recoverable in memory as a shell on a beach.

"Lucie," Elias whispered.

The figure of Lucie walked up the lawn toward the house, then disappeared along the garden path that led to the kitchen door. Elias sat down on the bed, his heart pounding. He put on his bathrobe, then sat down again. It *was* Lucie, he knew. Through time, through space, through imagination, she had somehow come to him, how he didn't know, but assuredly he was awake, not dreaming. She had come to him, just as she'd promised so long ago. Time could somehow be redeemed, and the wonder of that brought tears to Elias's eyes. He heard the kitchen door open. He thought he had locked it, but perhaps not. On this night, all things were possible: memory could be mistaken as well as recaptured. Elias rose to look at himself in the mirror.

I've changed since Paris, he thought, touching the lines of his cheek. He had resisted this knowledge, he knew. He touched his graying hair, then carefully combed it. He wondered whether or not to dress, then decided he would put his maroon smoking jacket over his pajamas. Elias splashed shaving lotion on his neck, his cheeks; he stroked his eyes to press out the wrinkles. He looked younger, he thought. From below he heard footsteps in the living room. Should he go meet her? Elias reached for the door and partially opened it. He hesitated, then sat in the wing chair by the door. He folded his hands in his lap. He would wait for her. He would prepare himself.

The telephone by the bedside rang. For a moment Elias thought not to pick it up. Then he did. At first he heard nothing, neither the sea sound nor the faraway music. "Hello?" he said. Then he heard a voice also saying "Hello" so that he thought he was hearing his echo. "Elias?" the voice said. "Is that you? It's Gérard."

"Gérard," Elias repeated dumbly. "But you're dead."

The voice, which now he did recognize as Gérard's, laughed. "How can I be dead? I'm talking to you this very moment."

"I—I hadn't heard from you ... I thought ... I thought your spirit visited me one night years ago."

"Where? In that state of yours—Connecticut?" Gérard pronounced it badly, so that Elias had to smile. "That would be a good trick."

"I—it's just—how are you, Gérard?" Elias asked. "Where are you?"

"This is the first time we have ever spoken on the telephone, my friend, do you know that? Never in all the time in Paris did we speak on the telephone."

"We didn't have any telephones," Elias said.

"Ah—I forgot. There's the reason."

"How are you, Gérard?" Elias asked again. He heard footsteps on the stairs. "I'm just so surprised to hear from you."

"Time goes faster than one can ever imagine," Gérard said. "One day you're a young man with no money in your pocket, the next day you have grandchildren and are handing out *sucettes*. But listen, Elias. I must speak quickly. I'm calling because you are in great danger."

"Danger? What do you mean?"

"I can't tell you exactly. But believe me, please. I have become sensitive to such things. I have felt it strongly these past months. You are in danger. Be attentive."

"Gérard, what? How do you know?"

"Elias, be careful," Gérard said. "Be—" And then his voice was obscured by the rising of the familiar sea sound.

Elias replaced the receiver on the hook. He heard Lucie's footsteps slowly coming down the hall. He moved quickly and closed the bedroom door. The footsteps paused. Elias locked the door, went back to the bed, and listened. The steps resumed, more hurried now, and stopped in front of the door. The knob turned.

"Go away!" Elias shouted. The knob rattled, then the entire door shook. "Go away!" he cried again. Now it seemed as if the whole house were shaking, so hard that Elias feared it might crumble around him. The children's song ran through his head like a speeded-up record: "Ashesashesweallfall-down." Elias sobbed with fear. Whoever—whatever—was outside the door moaned, a low animalistic moan passionate in its longing and loss. As he had done once before, Elias dove deep under the covers, hands over his ears to blot out the sound. "Go away, go away," he said over and over, the words an incantation against the horror that had come for him. The wailing ceased; the house once again was still. Strangely, Elias fell asleep.

When he awoke, cramped and stiff, the light was as clear and blue as the thinnest eggshell. He felt quite cheery, the terror of the previous night gone. He looked out the window. Rain dripped from the trees. Mist rose off the pond in warm spirals. He would make coffee and fry an egg. He opened the door and looked down the hall: nothing was there. No marks were on the floor. Downstairs, the kitchen door was open, but the wind might have done that. He searched the house room by room, knowing he would find nothing. He picked up the kitchen phone: the dial tone was steady and strong. He would have the phones disconnected soon. Like electricity, it was another thing he could do without. His solitude would be all the more perfect. Elias put the coffee water on to boil. He was smiling, he realized.

As the coffee dripped, he turned to the classical station and heard the last part of Debussy's clarinet rhapsody. The announcer noted that Nadia Boulanger had died. Elias thought of the yellow building with the green shutters, closed then, closed now. Coffee in hand, he stepped outside into a day as fine as cut glass. Life would still be very much the same, he thought, and the same after that.

A little ways down the drive, he found Charles's body. His neck had been broken, and a deep gash ran down his side, exposing the liver, a portion of which had been pecked away. Elias fetched a shovel from the potato cellar, then put it back. He took the little dog's body down to the reflecting pool and rowed the swan boat to the middle. There he dropped Charles's body into the water. Elias waited for the ripples to subside and the pool once more become as smooth as polished stone. He spent the rest of the morning staring at the clouds above, and then—tiring of that—at their reflections on the now glassy surface, reflections that seemed to penetrate, but only artificially, to the depths below.

Comfort

*T*he two young women faced each other in their almost identical chairs and rocked. The early spring evening was warm, and they had opened the tall bay windows—the very reason they'd rented this apartment—to a small breeze and the scent of grass, which the landlord had just finished mowing. The chairs were white, wicker, and cheap. The young women had found them at a yard sale the previous summer, when they were furnishing the apartment. They'd joked then about drinking tea and rocking and growing old together by the bay windows, and so they had bought the chairs, in part to celebrate their friendship.

Their names were Laurie and Michaela. "Two good Irish lasses," an old boyfriend of Michaela's had called them. They'd liked that. Every now and then Michaela would break theatrically into "How Are Things in Glocca Morra?" or "When You and I Were Young, Maggie," and they would laugh.

Neither had any Irish blood at all. Laurie, however, considered herself at least mystically Irish. Listening to a Celtic
folk lament, the concertina or fiddle stately and low, often
brought tears to her eyes. She was the smaller of the two,
with strawberry-blond hair that curled in ways that she de-
spised: she envied Michaela's straight, almost Spanish-looking
black hair, which still hung well below her shoulders. Laurie
kept hers short in an effort to manage the hated curls. She
thought of herself as small and clumsy—"graceless" was a
word that occurred to her—whereas the one word she thought
of for Michaela was "long": long not only in body but in
movement, "long" meaning languorous, sinewy, effortless.

They had met their senior year at Skidmore and quickly
became friends, which surprised Laurie, since she was certain
she had already found all the friends she would ever have.
Neither knowing exactly what she wanted to do after grad-
uation, they decided to linger in Saratoga another year. Michaela worked as an assistant to the director of the College
Artists Series, while Laurie clerked in a used-book store. Michaela talked vaguely about going to New York in the fall to
work for a theatrical producer or a talent agency; she also
talked about traveling for a year in Europe. "You should make
some plans," Laurie would tell her, and then feel foolish,
because she herself had no plans. Besides, Michaela's waiting
seemed more like a resting, a gathering of strength: it was all
she wanted and needed for now.

"Maybe we should just take in men," Michaela said once,
to which Laurie replied that they would probably still be
living together, spinsters, when they were eighty.

But this spring evening they weren't thinking about any of

this. To celebrate the heat they put on long dresses that clung loosely to their skin, drank Tom Collinses, and rocked and waited for Laurie's mother's boyfriend to arrive for dinner.

Her mother had called three nights ago from New York. Ted was coming to Saratoga to direct a television spot for the Summer Music Festival: could Laurie possibly have him over one night, since he'd be all alone at the motel and would love to see her and have a home-cooked meal? Laurie was sure he didn't care one way or another about seeing her— they hardly knew each other, after all—and as for home-cooked meals, she and Michaela never had any, being content to heat up frozen diet dinners or make quick salads with whatever vegetables were wilting in the refrigerator. But she agreed, and dutifully called Ted at the Plum Tree Inn. He sounded pleased to hear from her, and accepted the invitation.

"Is this one going to last?" Michaela asked, as they rocked. She had always followed Laurie's mother's affairs with interest.

Laurie shrugged. "Who knows? It's been going on for almost a year now. For Mom, that's a long time." She bit a fingernail. "Anyway, I hope so. She'd gotten real cynical before she met Ted. She didn't see anybody for *months.*"

"Who was before him? The Argentine?"

"No, the Conrail lawyer. Same difference. Both jerks."

"She's had an interesting love life, your mother," Michaela said. She yawned, and draped her legs over the arm of the rocker. "I admire her for that."

"To tell you the truth," Laurie said, "I think she could've done without a lot of it."

"But this guy's good, huh?"

Laurie sighed. "He treats her well enough, I guess. She says she can talk with Ted in a way she's never been able to before. She says it's just comfortable with him."

"Comfortable," Michaela repeated thoughtfully.

"I don't trust him, though," Laurie said.

Michaela looked at her. "Why not?"

"I think he'd cheat on her. Maybe he does. He seems like the kind of guy who likes to play around."

"Now what makes you say that?"

Laurie shrugged. "It's just the way he looks at you."

"Oh? At *you*?"

Laurie was uncomfortable. "I went to the shore with them for a day last summer. And I could feel him—looking at me. He kept it cool, you know. But I could see him sneaking glances."

"Well, what's so strange about that? He didn't come on to you, did he?"

"Oh, no."

"Did you want him to?"

"Michaela! He's my mother's boyfriend."

"Listen—" Michaela sat up in the chair and crossed her legs in her lap. She was grinning mischievously. "Why don't you try and seduce him? Just to find out?"

"Not a good idea, Michaela," Laurie said.

"You're such a prude."

They both broke into laughter.

"On second thought," Michaela said brightly, "it's probably better that I do it. It's less complicated that way."

"That makes sense," Laurie agreed.

"I'm always thinking about you." And they laughed again.

"Wait!" Michaela held up her hand. "Friendship only goes

so far!" She narrowed her eyes, a mock sleuth. "Is he good-looking? I gotta know before I commit."

"Oh, positively," Laurie said. "Positively good-looking." She paused. "For his age, of course."

"Well, that settles it then," Michaela said with feigned relief. She glanced at her watch. "One thing's for sure—punctual he's not. He was supposed to be here twenty minutes ago." She settled deeper into her chair, closed her eyes, and rocked.

She's so calm, Laurie thought. *If I came back next week, next month, she could still be here, eyes still closed.* For a moment Laurie saw Michaela as a man might, could feel her calm almost as a sensuality that offered refuge yet promised nothing—and was the more exciting for that. She realized with both envy and pride that Michaela would turn out all right in life, that whatever she chose to do, she—unlike Laurie—would have an easy time of it. She had a grace and an ease, and that ease would command not only attention—especially from men—but also willingness. *She will be served,* Laurie thought, *and she'll never need to ask.*

The buzzer rang.

"Him," Michaela said.

Laurie nodded. "Him." She rose.

At the door they embraced awkwardly, and he might have kissed her lightly on the cheek. "Ted," she said. She could smell aftershave and soap. *This is what he smelled like at the beach,* she recalled, *or in the car driving there.*

"I'm late, I'm late," he said, grinning sheepishly. His brown hair, cut in a way that "looks Roman," as her mother put it, was still damp from the shower. He wore jeans and a blue chambray work shirt, and wasn't wearing the gold necklace that Laurie had once seen, for which she was glad. Michaela would look down on that, and somehow, even if she didn't entirely like Ted, Laurie wanted Michaela to approve of him. He was, after all, her mother's boyfriend.

"I'm sorry," he said. He handed her a bottle of wine, much more expensive than the ones she had bought. "We were out in the boondocks scouting a mountain stream, and the art director didn't like any of my locations, so we had to keep tramping around." He put his arm around her shoulder as they walked into the room. "So—I was late to begin with, and then I got lost coming over. This town can't have more than three streets, and I get lost!" He waved hello to Michaela. "I thought about calling, and then I thought, hell, by the time I find a phone, I could probably find the place, and—"

"It's okay," Laurie said. "We were just sitting here."

Ted grinned at her. "Well, you look as gorgeous as ever."

Laurie introduced him to Michaela, and they shook hands.

"Why a mountain stream?" Michaela asked.

"Because one of the shots in the storyboard calls for a violinist in a tuxedo to be fiddling in the middle of a stream." Ted shook his head and laughed. "You wouldn't believe the nonsense I go through!"

Laurie brought glasses of wine. She and Michaela sat in the wicker chairs, with Ted across from them on the sofa. He stretched out his legs and sighed. "You don't know how good it is just to sit," he said.

"You know, it's actually hot in here," Michaela said. "The first time this spring." She rose and stood by the opened bay windows; the scent of grass and trillium filled the room. Ted sneezed, and sneezed again.

"Hay fever," he said. He took a tissue from a small pack

in his pocket and blew his nose. "Grass. Every spring." He sneezed again.

"They just mowed the lawn," Laurie said.

"I'll close the windows," Michaela offered.

Ted waved his hand. "It's okay. It's really not that bad yet. Tramping through those damn woods probably didn't help either." He stifled yet another sneeze. "You can have the country, as far as I'm concerned."

"Saratoga isn't exactly the country," Laurie said.

"To me it is. I'll take the city any day. The best thing about concrete is that it doesn't pollinate."

Michaela closed the windows.

"So how's Mom?" Laurie asked.

"Fine, fine. She's fine." Ted carefully placed his wineglass on the arm of the sofa. "She's working really hard right now. Her company's setting up that trade show in Westchester, you know."

"Oh, she told me about that."

"Do you direct movies, too?" Michaela asked. *The way she holds her wineglass,* Laurie thought. *So gently. Almost as if she weren't holding it at all.*

"You mean like at the theaters?" Ted shook his head. "I do some industrial films. Business films. But mostly it's TV spots."

"Propaganda," Laurie said.

"Sure." He laughed. "I guess."

"I think commercials are some of the best things on TV," Michaela said. "They're better than the shows sometimes."

"Everybody says that," Laurie said.

"Well, it's true."

"They're still propaganda."

"They pay the bills," Ted said. "You wouldn't have TV without them. You wouldn't have business without them."

"Maybe that wouldn't be so bad," Laurie said.

"Laurie, don't sound like such a *throwback,*" Michaela said. "You sound like something left over from the sixties."

"I just think—" Laurie began, and then fell silent. *Why am I saying all this?* she wondered. *It was silly and it was stupid.* She looked at Ted. He sipped his wine and smiled at her.

"It must be exciting to direct a film," Michaela said. "Even a TV spot."

Ted shrugged. "Not really. It's a lot like the Army—you know, hurry up and wait. You're either waiting around for things to get set up or you're rushing to get a shot in before the light's gone. Or before the crew has to go into overtime."

"Could we watch this commercial being shot?" Michaela asked. "Could we get on the set?"

"I don't see why not," Ted said. Then he looked thoughtful. "Well, actually, it's fine by me, but this art director—I've never worked with him before, and he's a little wired. I better run it by him first."

"I thought you were the director," Laurie said.

"I am."

"Well, aren't you the boss?"

Ted smiled. "The art director is from the ad agency. He hired me. It's his show, really. And he likes to get involved. But I'll ask, if you want." He looked at each of them in turn.

"Oh, that would be great," Michaela said. "Wouldn't it, Laurie?"

"Sure," Laurie said, without enthusiasm.

They talked about other things then, and with her second

glass of wine Laurie felt more at ease. Soon they all crowded into the tiny kitchen. Michaela steamed broccoli and cut vegetables for the salad, while Ted happily crushed garlic and basted the French bread. Laurie burned herself testing the pasta for doneness. The kitchen was filled with steam and pungent cooking smells. She opened a window, and Ted began sneezing again. He went to his car for hay-fever pills.

"He's nice," Michaela said.

"He's smooth." Laurie stirred the pasta. "He's slick."

"And he *is* good-looking."

Laurie looked at her through the steam. "So you like him?"

"Sure," Michaela said. "Why not?"

Laurie opened the cupboard and took out three dinner plates. "Whatever possessed you to ask about visiting the set?"

"I think it'd be interesting," Michaela said. "Don't you?"

"No."

"Laurie!" Michaela laughed. "Aren't you curious at all?"

When Ted returned, they took their plates into the front room and sat on the rug. Michaela lit candles. *As if this were her house,* Laurie thought, *and she was the hostess, and I was just another visitor.* Ted entertained them with stories about disasters that happened on film shoots—trained cats that refused to respond on cue, crew meals that were delivered to the wrong town, spectacular sunsets that didn't materialize and spectacular rainstorms that did. Softened by the candlelight, he seemed much younger, Laurie thought: his hair shone, and his skin glowed. *He is good-looking,* she decided. Michaela was right. They opened another bottle of wine. Laurie felt light-headed. Looking across at Ted and Michaela, she fantasized that she was a very young child and they were her parents. Somewhere a music box was playing. In a moment they would tell her it was time for bed, and off she'd go, trailing her favorite blanket—

Michaela's laugh startled her.

"—but this art director," Ted was saying, "*insisted* that a talking seal really existed—"

"Seals don't talk," Laurie interrupted.

"Laurie! Haven't you been listening?" Michaela asked.

"This one had been around people so much that supposedly it did," Ted explained to her. He turned back to Michaela. "Anyway, so there I was, calling up every zoo and aquarium in the country to see if they knew anything about a talking seal. And do you know what they all told me? Each and every one?" He lightly touched Michaela's arm. "Seals—don't—talk!"

They burst into laughter, and Laurie joined in. For some reason she couldn't stop. "The things—" she sputtered. "The things—" She waved her hand helplessly. Michaela and Ted smiled, urging her along.

"The things—you have to do—for *Art,*" she gasped. And laughed even harder. Michaela looked at her quizzically. Ted twirled his wineglass by the stem, stared into it, and then refilled it.

"Sometimes I don't know why a grown man does these things," he said quietly. "Talking to seals. Arguing which way bears should run around the cereal box. Left to right, or"— he pointed with his finger—"right to left."

"It's business, Ted—American business," Laurie said.

"It must be exciting, though, too," Michaela said.

Ted looked up. "Sometimes it's just boring. And that's all. Do you know what I mean?" He sipped his wine.

"Everything gets boring," Laurie said. "Life's boring."

"Just ignore her," Michaela said to Ted. "She's going through some existentialist phase."

"No, I'm not," Laurie said. "Why did you say that?" She looked at Ted. "I don't know why she said that." Surprised by her anger, she rose and went unsteadily into the kitchen. She filled the sink with hot water and soap, too much of it. Bubbles rose in thick, foamy clusters. She thrust her hands into them and then began loudly piling pots into the sink. She tossed in some utensils and watched them disappear under the foam.

Michaela came in. "So—" Laurie said, not looking at her.

"Get nice. Lighten up."

"Look—just don't talk about my existentialist phase, okay? Or my sixties throwback phase, okay?"

"What is *wrong* with you this evening?" Michaela demanded.

"Just don't sound so—pompous," Laurie said.

Michaela sighed. "Laurie, why don't you give us all a break?"

"You and him both, huh?"

"Yes."

Laurie saluted. "Okay, Mom."

Michaela stared at her and then walked out. Laurie washed a few pots and emptied the sink. She took two deep breaths. *Get nice,* she told herself. She pursed her lips and then pulled her mouth into a tight, strained grin, the tendons along the side of her neck stretched taut. Water gurgled in the drain.

She returned to the front room. Ted was sitting cross-legged on the floor beside Michaela's rocker. They were talking quietly. *Like old friends,* Laurie thought. They looked up as she came in.

"Hi," Laurie said. "I'm back." She sat in the other rocker.

"We've been talking about where we'd go if we could go anywhere on earth," Michaela said. "Ted was saying he'd go to Patmos."

"It's a Greek island near Turkey," Ted said. "It's where John wrote the Book of Revelations."

"Just imagine that," Michaela said. She stretched, fingers interlocked and arms extended above her head so that her breasts were outlined against her dress. She draped one leg over the rocker; the skirt fell away, revealing a bare, brown leg. She delicately unstrapped her sandals and let them fall.

"When I was on Crete two summers ago," she said, "I used to go to a nude beach and spend the whole day there. I'd only get dressed to go to the taverna. Otherwise I was naked all day."

"I was at one of those beaches too," Ted said. "Maybe I saw you."

"Were you naked too?"

Ted laughed.

"Remember those little old ladies who rent you beach umbrellas?" Michaela asked. "Did they have them on your beach?"

Ted nodded.

"They were always dressed in black," Michaela said. "Black dresses, black leather shoes. They must've been so hot."

"They must've gotten a lot of sand in their shoes," Ted said.

"Right!"

"I wonder what they thought," Laurie said.

"About what?" Michaela asked.

"About all those naked bodies on their beach."

Michaela looked puzzled.

"*Their* beach," Laurie said. "Get it?"

Michaela looked at her. In the candlelight her eyes seemed like embers brushed by the breeze.

"They were probably glad to have somebody to rent their umbrellas to," Ted said.

"Were they black too, Michaela?" Laurie pressed. "The umbrellas?" *I'm sorry,* she thought. *I'll stop.*

"Yes. They were," Michaela said slowly. "Black beach umbrellas. On white sand." She held Laurie's gaze. "With a blue sea. And blue sky. In case you're interested."

They fell silent. For the first time that spring Laurie heard crickets. Ted poured them all another glass of wine. Michaela considered hers and then put it down.

"I'll tell you another story about Crete," she said. "I've never told this to anyone before." She looked at Laurie. "Not even to you."

"It was one of those days when the wind blows hot early in the morning, but later everything gets real calm and quiet. I decided to bike along the coast and maybe go for a swim. After a couple of hours I stopped for lunch. I hid my bike behind some bushes and went down the hill to the beach below. It was a little cove, really, with rocks on either side. You couldn't see the road from down there, and if you went over by the rocks, nobody above could see you. I spread out my towel, took off my shorts and shirt—I had my swimsuit on underneath—and went for a swim. Then I ate lunch. I remember exactly what I had: some figs, an orange, and a roll from breakfast."

"I love those Greek figs," Ted said.

"It was real hot and still. The only thing I could hear was these little waves lapping on the sand. I got sleepy. I took off my top. And then I thought, what the hell, nobody can see, so I took off the bottom too. And I went to sleep."

"I could never do that," Laurie said. "I'd be afraid somebody would see."

"I had a dream," Michaela continued. "I dreamed I was there on the beach, and it had gotten real windy. The waves were running high and white-tipped, even though the sky was still clear and blue. I looked out to sea, and, as I was looking, a white sailboat rose up out of the waves and came crashing toward me. When it was about forty yards offshore, it swung around, so that the sails were just flapping—"

"Luffing," Ted corrected.

"—luffing. I could see that nobody was on board. And I thought, *Now how could a boat sail by itself?* But it just stayed there, bobbing in the waves. And then I realized it was there to pick me up. It was *mine,* somehow. I got frightened, and I woke up."

She paused dramatically. "And there, not far away, I saw a boy sitting on one of the rocks, looking at me—"

"Uh-oh," Ted said, and Laurie tittered.

"I didn't know where he'd come from or how long he'd been there. He was about twelve years old or so. He had black hair and the most beautiful olive skin, and he was wearing blue cotton shorts. His legs were smooth, almost hairless. He didn't seem at all bothered that I'd woken up. He just kept sitting there, staring at me."

"And you're naked, right?" Ted asked.

Michaela nodded.

"Michaela, weren't you embarrassed?" Laurie asked.

"No." She shook her head. "I don't know why. Maybe because he didn't seem to be. He just kept looking at me as if I were something that had washed up on the beach. He didn't say or do anything, and neither did I."

She sipped her wine and then pulled her knees to her chin, like a child. "I mean, he was just a boy," she said.

"So what happened?" Ted asked.

Michaela hesitated a moment. "He stood up, finally. I thought he was going to go. But he didn't. Instead, he—" she looked at Laurie. "I've never told you this, you know— he pulled down his shorts—"

"Michaela—" Laurie breathed.

"—they were just elastic-banded, no belt, a boy's pants. He pulled them down, and I could see that he was erect—"

"Oh, no," Laurie said.

"—and he began to masturbate."

"No!"

"—right in front of me. Staring at me the whole time, as if I'd disappear."

Ted laughed nervously.

"I don't believe this," Laurie cried.

"It's true," Michaela said.

"So—I mean—what did you do?" Ted asked. His voice seemed thicker, harsher.

"I just watched." Michaela rested her cheek against her knee and looked at him. "In a funny way, it was as if he were doing it for me, too. His hand just moved faster and faster, and then he closed his eyes, and moaned a little, and then he—you know—spilled, all over the sand."

Ted grunted. Laurie closed her eyes.

"What happened after that?" Ted asked.

"Nothing. He pulled up his shorts and walked up the hill. Believe it or not, I fell asleep again. And when I woke up, I honestly didn't know if I'd dreamed it all. So I went over to where he'd been standing, and yes, there was his—semen— on the sand. I put my finger in it and felt it. Just to be sure."

Laurie's head was swimming. Far down the street a car sputtered, coughed, came to life, and then died again, leaving them in silence.

"That's an amazing story," Ted murmured.

Michaela stretched languorously, and yawned. Laurie felt adrift, cast aside by a wave she had failed to catch, a wave already breaking farther in, ashore.

"Let's call Mom!" she cried. "Wouldn't you like to talk to Mom, Ted?"

He had been looking at Michaela, but now turned to her. "It's late, Laurie," he said.

"No—she'll be awake," Laurie pleaded. "C'mon. We could all talk to her."

Ted shook his head. "Not tonight."

"Don't you want to talk to her, Ted?" A trace of panic was in her voice. She rose and stumbled against the coffee table, knocking over the wine bottle, still a quarter full. "Oh, no—" she moaned.

"Don't worry," Michaela said. "I'll take care of it."

Where am I going? Laurie wondered. She walked over to the bay windows and stared out. "Stars," she announced, and they seemed to be swirling, both outside and inside her head. When she turned again, Michaela and Ted were staring at her. *They hate me,* Laurie thought.

"I'm going to my room now," she said thickly. "It's late." She fell on her bed without undressing.

When she awoke, the apartment was quiet. She rose, still dizzy, her mouth dry. She groped for the bedroom door. The front room was dark: Ted was gone. Michaela's sandals were still by the rocker. Laurie could smell the wine she had tipped over. She went into the kitchen and drank two glasses of water and then returned to the front room. From the bay windows she saw that a thick, fibrous fog had transformed the trees into ghosts and the streetlights into soft, haloed moons.

Michaela should see this, she thought. For one strange moment she considered waking her. And then from behind her friend's closed door she heard Ted sneeze.

As quietly as she could, Laurie walked back to her room. She lay down. She wanted to think and she wanted to sleep. She slept.

When she woke again, the fog had disappeared and the sun was burning off the dew. The air smelled woody and musty. Her head ached terribly. She went into the front room: Michaela's door was open now, and Laurie could see her— alone—curled in sleep, fist to her mouth like a child. Laurie softly closed the door and picked up the glasses and wine bottles. She sponged where the wine had spilled. She filled the sink with hot, soapy water and took two aspirins. Then she returned to the front room and dialed the Plum Tree Inn.

"Mr. Ted Bremmer's room, please," she told the switchboard.

He picked up on the third ring. "Yes?" he said, groggily.

"Fuck you," Laurie said, and hung up.

She finished doing the dishes and then made some coffee, started to drink it, and thought she would retch. She ate an untoasted English muffin and felt better. Using the last of the milk, she made another cup of coffee. *Michaela will want some when she gets up,* she thought, and so brewed a fresh pot. She reread the previous day's paper.

Later she heard Michaela enter the bathroom. The shower ran for a long time, and then Michaela came into the kitchen in her robe, her long hair stringy and wet. She grunted when she saw the coffee, and poured a cup, holding it with both hands as if it might fall.

"No more milk," Laurie said. "You'll have to drink it black."

Michaela nodded.

"Hangover?"

Michaela shook her head. "Just tired. I can't seem to wake up."

"Ah," Laurie said.

Michaela blew on her coffee. "Thanks for doing the dishes," she said. "I would've helped."

Laurie waved her hand.

"So—how do *you* feel?" Michaela asked. "You drank a lot last night."

"Fine, fine," Laurie said. "Thanks for asking." She folded the newspaper and carefully put it beside the table. "Want to do something today?"

Michaela looked up from her coffee cup. "Like what?"

Laurie shrugged.

"I don't feel like doing anything today except sitting," Michaela said. "And I wish there was some milk."

"We can get some later," Laurie said. She scratched her fingernail on the tablecloth, back and forth, over and over, deepening the line.

"So—" she said.

Michaela glanced up. "So?"

"So how was it? Ted and"—her voice caught—"and all?"

Michaela sighed. "He was so guilty. He kept making me promise not to tell you."

Laurie laughed harshly. "Well, now you did, didn't you? So much for that promise."

"Laurie—you knew anyway, didn't you?"

"Oh, sure." She stopped scratching the tablecloth. "I just can't believe it. You really did do it, didn't you?"

Michaela didn't reply.

"Was that true last night?" Laurie asked. "That story you told?"

Michaela smiled. "No—of course not. I made it up."

"I thought so!" Laurie cried. "I said so, didn't I?" She shook her head. "I could've told him. I could've *insisted*—"

"But you weren't sure," Michaela interrupted. "Were you?"

Laurie was silent.

"Laurie—" Michaela took her hand. "Laurie—listen. You wanted me to. We talked—remember?"

Laurie pulled her hand away. "We were joking!"

Michaela shook her head.

"We were! Don't say we weren't."

"You wanted me to," Michaela repeated.

"I didn't! How can—how can you *twist* this?" But Laurie was confused: she wasn't sure now what they'd said before Ted came. "Listen—if—if—" she felt she was losing her breath, as if her words might choke her—"if my mother— ever finds out about this—"

"Laurie, why should she?"

"—I'll kill you."

Michaela laughed. "Okay, sure."

"No, I mean it," Laurie said. "I'll kill you. I really will."

Michaela stopped smiling. "Laurie, how would she ever find out?"

"I know you," Laurie murmured.

"Let's go sit in the front room, okay?" Michaela suggested gently. "Let's go have our coffee in there."

They sat in the facing wicker chairs. Michaela began to rock, and Laurie watched her.

"Isn't this nice?" Michaela said. "I think this is all I really want to do today, don't you? I just don't want to think about anything else." She closed her eyes. Outside, Laurie heard birds chattering, and from somewhere—although she knew she only imagined it—the sound of a receding sea.

"Well, now we know about him, don't we?" Michaela said. "What we wondered about, remember?"

"Yes," Laurie said.

"But we'll never, never tell." Eyes still closed, Michaela spoke as if to a child.

"That's right," Laurie said.

Michaela stopped rocking. "But at least *we* know, don't we?" She looked at Laurie, and her smile was dark and cold and triumphant. "That's sort of a comfort, isn't it?"

For a complete list of books available from Penguin in the United States, write to Dept. DG, Penguin Books, 299 Murray Hill Parkway, East Rutherford, New Jersey 07073.

For a complete list of books available from Penguin in Canada, write to Penguin Books Canada Limited, 2801 John Street, Markham, Ontario L3R 1B4.